Margot Schlumm
Oktober 1960

Yesterday

a novel by MARIA DERMOÛT

TRANSLATED FROM THE DUTCH
BY HANS KONINGSBERGER

SIMON AND SCHUSTER · 1959
NEW YORK

This novel was originally published in Holland
under the title *Nog Pas Gisteren.*

LIBRARY OF CONGRESS CATALOG CARD NUMBER: 59–11192
MANUFACTURED IN THE UNITED STATES OF AMERICA
BY KINGSPORT PRESS, INC., KINGSPORT, TENN.

Teach us to care and not to care
　　　　　　　　　　—T. S. ELIOT

ON THE ISLAND OF JAVA, between the mountains Lawu and Wilis but closer to the Lawu, deep in a walled garden under dark-green trees, stood the house.

The house was called "the big house," and there they lived: Rick, her parents, and the servants.

In the harsh light of day and from the outside it was an ugly house, whitewashed, with wide borders of black tar, dull gray blinds, the tiled roof all sagging and weather-beaten; in the evening it still looked like something. But inside, the house was always beautiful and silent, and very cool.

Two carriage drives led up to it. One was lined with royal palms, straight and slender and haughty; they didn't give much shade with their smooth, yellow trunks and narrow leaves waving in the wind. The other drive, the old one, was bordered by kanari trees, which kept it moist and dusky green all through the long sultry day.

In front of the house was a large lawn, with a stiff prickly aloe in the center of it and a border of pink crocuses around it.

On each side a row of white marble steps curved from the garden up to the front veranda, which had a marble floor; the white floor was inlaid with a large seven-pointed star, in black.

Fat round plastered pillars with square bases and capitals supported the roof over the veranda in front. Then came an inner gallery, beyond it a closed gallery with four rooms in a row on each side, and then again—as in the front—an open veranda with stone pillars and steps leading to the garden. The slatted gray doors inside the house were never closed, and against the draft there were screens made of black silk, which squeaked on their hinges when someone went from one room to another. They came from Singapore, and there were golden cranes embroidered on the silk. But the glory of the house was its floor.

The verandas and the galleries all had the same white marble floor. The daily scrubbing and mopping, and perhaps age too, had worn the marble smooth; it no longer looked stark white and hard as it had once, but was wax-colored and gleaming and almost transparent. It made the large rooms seem silent and shimmering—as if it were not a floor but a shallow pond.

And everything in the rooms stood reflected in it, motionless and vague: the black and gold screens, the brown teakwood furniture, the bright-yellow lamp shades, the green of the plants. In the evening the golden circles of light from the oil lamps lay quietly on the white marble. When someone passed along a gallery, a tinted shadow flitted across the floor lightly.

All the walls were whitewashed; all the woodwork, including the ceiling, was painted gray.

Rick's father, Papa, was a tall man, slender, with a dark goatee and dark gray eyes. He spoke softly, and sometimes he would laugh suddenly—no one liked that—and he could also get very excited and angry about things. Mama was rather short and a bit heavy, which was a pity. She wore her springy brown hair in a stiff knot pinned up high, with a curly bang in front. She had pretty light-brown eyes.

Rick loved her parents, but not very much really. They were always together; she didn't belong with them. But when Papa was out, in the cane fields or at the sugar mill, Mama was alone, and for her.

In the mornings Mama walked around in a light-blue sarong smelling of batik wax, a white jacket with lace edges, and slippers of velvet decorated with golden paillettes. She made the rounds through the house and the garden, very busily, and Rick went along, hanging on her arm or carrying her key basket. They went to the storeroom, the stables, saw all the animals, the laundryman, the seamstress, they arranged flowers, cooked a pudding—and then suddenly Rick was given some school work to do and was sent to the schoolroom in the guest pavilion.

A large oblong map of Java hung on the wall there. It was a beautiful map; the sea was blue and all the mountains were blue too.

There were also a blackboard and a bell, but these were never used. Outside the window, deer stepped around in the grass. When Rick leaned out the window they first sniffed nervously, then came closer and nosed her hand to see if she had something nice to offer; sometimes they licked her fingers.

Later her work had to be checked. When she made only a few mistakes Mama said that she was "very pleased" with Rick. Papa never said anything; he always told her that one must be ambitious in life, that she should take pride in doing her tasks well without praise or reward. Rick would look at him silently then. But usually he came home late from the fields—well past noon—and was very tired. His rumpled suit had large dark stains where it stuck to his body, and his white duck shoes were dusty, or full of mud if it had been raining.

On the open veranda at the back of the house stood an easy chair—he always collapsed in it immediately, pale and perspiring. He held his white topee in one hand, and in the other a handkerchief with which he dabbed his face. Mama and one of the servants stood there, waiting to help, but no one was to move until the beo gave the sign. The beo was a little bird, gleamingly black with an orange beak, and it lived in a bamboo cage standing next to the easy chair. The beo could talk. First it watched with clever round little eyes, its head held sideways, and then it suddenly began in a gay, sharp voice.

"Come on, pull off the master's shoes, quick, quick, pull off the master's shoes, quick-quick-quick!" It spoke Malayan. Papa laughed, the second houseboy pulled off his shoes and took them along to whiten them with pipe clay, the topee too. Mama gave Papa his slippers, and then they went inside. The beo stared after them.

Early in the morning the blinds for the doors and windows had been closed; on the outer verandas green-and-white-striped shades had been lowered between the pillars. Now it was cool and quiet in the high rooms, the floors shone, freshly cut flowers stood everywhere. Voices came from only one room, their voices together. Papa's voice was often loud and angry when he came home from the fields so tired, and Mama's voice was soothing.

Then they had to eat rijsttafel, and have a rest, and get up again, and shower, and dress.

About four o'clock, as soon as the worst heat had passed, the sluice gate in the river was closed and all the ditches in the garden were filled with water. The garden boys and the water carriers went around watering the plants and the lawns, and it smelled as if it had been raining, of dark wet earth.

Papa had to go to the mill now, and Rick and Mama had tea on the front veranda, rocking gently in their chairs because of the heat. A little later they went for a drive. Mangun, the first houseboy, came to ask which horses the coachman should hitch up, and Mama said the black team, or the brown, or the dappled—each had its turn. When Papa came home early he sometimes went too, or he walked in the garden with Mama and Jimmy, the ape.

Always the same way: he put his hand on Mama's arm —he was much taller than she—and with the other hand held the ape. Mama walked a bit stiffly, sideways, and she looked straight ahead because she didn't want to look at the ape and she didn't want the ape to look at her: they disliked each other intensely. Jim liked only Papa; Papa sometimes spoke to him and the ape moved his lips, but no sound came out.

It darkened early, a short twilight, and the grass, the bushes and the trees in the garden became such a sharp, such a yellowish green. Little bats flitted about. The Lawu, the big mountain behind the house, lay wide and restful in the evening, at times purple, at times the darkest of blues, at times reddish from the setting sun; and here and there the first golden stars began to shine in the sky.

Frogs began to croak; crickets and grasshoppers, mosquitoes and beetles and all the other insects started to buzz, to chirp, to squeak, to hum and to whistle softly. Bats and night birds chirped. First it was as if they were practicing— they tried for a second, then came to a frightened halt, and only when it had become really dark did their sound come regularly and without stopping: the chorus of thousands, thousands of little voices in the dark and speechless night. Then the lamps were lit, their gleam reflected in the floor; a coolness blew from the mountain through the house and stirred the lace curtains. Rick had to practice on the piano and eat before the others.

Many evenings guests came, or visits were paid. All the lamps on the front veranda were lit for visitors. If they were people from the mill, they came on foot, and a servant with a lantern guided them through the garden. If they came from farther away, a carriage drove up along one of the drives and around the lawn, two yellow lights, the sound of hoofs and the squeak of wheels on the pebbles in the dark.

Papa and Mama stood at the top of the marble stairs, all dressed up. Sometimes Papa would go down and help a lady get out of a carriage, then bring her up on his arm and talk and laugh with her. He did that only for someone he liked.

Rick just stood and looked at him. He was so handsome and tall in his white suit, he looked like someone out of a book. She had to shake hands with the guests and then go away again.

Or another time her parents would drive out, to one of the other sugar mills, or to the town, to a party. Then Mama wore one of her three best dresses.

Rick stayed home alone; she ate at the large table and Mangun, the first houseboy, served her, but the boy who took care of the lamps was always in a hurry and he started turning down the other lamps and blowing them out with a long tin tube.

Suddenly the house was so big, and without much light left, the black trees in the garden stood silent and close around it, the two carriage drives—who could be sure someone wasn't sneaking along in the dark out there? But then the night watchmen came, one for the front, one for the back, and they took turns at the sides of the house.

And in the meantime Papa and Mama drove through the night in their carriage, Mama in a dress of yellow silk with a fan made of feathers, and a diamond flower on a velvet choker around her neck, and Papa next to her in evening clothes, black and white, with a high collar. He had a fan, too, a little black one. Every now and again they said something to each other. Rick could see them clearly in the carriage, and also the coachman and the groom on the box. The two horses trotted, they snorted in the cold air and shook their heads, and the leather harnesses creaked softly and regularly. In the carriage lanterns tall white candles burned.

It was pleasant to ride like that in the evening through the cool darkness, the moon shining perhaps—suppose they would drive on, not turn around, not come back— who would blame them?

She was glad when her old nurse, Urip, called her to come to bed.

"Now, immediately, do you hear!"

U RIP HAD BROUGHT HER MAT, her pillow, her sirih box and spittoon to Rick's bedroom. She had lit the night lamp, hunted for mosquitoes inside the curtains around the bed, and then tucked the nets back in. "You'd better go straight to bed," she always said, but Rick just leaned against the bed and looked at her sitting on the mat preparing her quid. Urip took out some sirih leaves and crushed them in her hand—they smelled so sharp that it made your mouth pucker—and added a piece of betel nut, a drop of lime, a bit of tobacco. She rubbed this mixture against her strong teeth which gleamed blackly, then pushed it into her cheek and started chewing. Her saliva became as red as blood.

"Talk a bit!" Rick said.

But Urip was old; she preferred to chew quietly, and it wasn't good to talk too much.

"Sleeping is better, heart of mine," she muttered with the quid in her cheek.

Rick had expected that. She went to one of the windows, lifted the latch and carefully pushed the blinds aside. Under the window, out on the open veranda, Karto sat every night. He was the first watchman, guarding the back of the house, and he sat on his mat next to the sewing table. He sat up straight, his legs crossed, a sarong around his shoulders against the coolness of the night, and he smoked cigarettes which he rolled himself. Next to him lay an old saber and a long, two-pronged wooden fork, to catch thieves. There was also a lantern, but it was never lit. The only light came from a gaudy Chinese lantern hanging from the veranda ceiling.

Rick climbed out of the window and sat down next to him in her own chair, an old decrepit rocking chair from Palembang, black lacquer with gold figures, which creaked in all its joints.

"Come, let's talk a bit!" she said, because Karto was always willing to talk.

He had been a porter once, that's why he was so strong. His feet were like two pieces of leather, flat and horny, because of the steepness of the mountain paths and the weight of the burdens on the bamboo yoke across his shoulders.

Every night.

There were many porters, even now, but he was no longer one of them. They had walked single file, with torches when there was no moon, past the lake and through the wood, and then around the cone of the mountain. There were no trees there, only the mountain and the wind, and they walked faster without speaking—because of the evil spirits—and never looked around. And the bamboo yokes went *kerret-tet-tet, kerret-tet-tet*—Karto could imitate that sound beautifully.

Every night.

The following morning they reached the other side of the mountain, with their loads of coffee or rice or whatever —*kerret-tet-tet, kerret-tet-tet*—no, they wouldn't get him to do that any more.

Or he talked about the others, although that wasn't quite proper.

"Listen, the first water carrier has borrowed money from the Chinese and when the Chinese comes he hides himself, just like Urip!" Karto laughed and was very pleased, because he didn't like Urip at all. "You watch! Urip—" he went on in a whisper, looking over his shoulder at the window—who had been so rich in her village, she once had a house and a garden with a wall around it, coconut palms, a well, a rice field, two water buffalos, a plow, a chest full of seed and one with clothes, and gold coins for buttons on her jacket.

"Rich, really!" Her relatives had lived there too, and her husband—actually his name was Urip—and the relatives of her husband, and then in a few years "gone, finished, swallowed up." He swept one of his large flat hands across the other. "Gone!"

Rick rocked in her chair and didn't answer. Urip had been her nurse long ago; she had been away all those years, and now she was back with her two little nieces, Assi and Nèng, who helped in the kitchen—Urip borrowing from the Chinese, and she had already received so much in advances on her wages; what was going to happen to her?

Karto didn't like the cook either.

"Such a skinflint, such a greedy miser!" Not a biscuit, not a piece of dried fish, not a cup of coffee, nothing, never. In the morning, after a long night, if Mangun didn't tell her to—"not a cup of coffee!"

"Women," Karto muttered, "either too much of everything or too little of everything, never just enough, as it should be!"

And the other night watchman wanted to go to Borneo to pan for gold; there was a lot of money in that. Not him. He would never go to Borneo to wash gold, because he was from the mountain—from around here, but from the mountain.

And the laundryman, with the long nail on one of his little fingers—tut tut!—had taken another wife, a young one, not into his house here at the back, of course, but outside, in the village; and now he was always fighting with his first wife and they both shouted so that everyone could hear them. Shouting wasn't good for anything!

The cowherd had taken that beautiful little boy of his to the grandparents, far away, because one of the Sultan's men had come to buy the child and he didn't want that.

"Why?" Rick asked. "Doesn't the Sultan have children of his own?"

"Oh yes—a hundred and ten of them—but he's always ready to buy a beautiful boy like that."

"Why, if he already has so many?"

"Just because . . . to play with . . ."

Then there was Rose, the seamstress. She was from Sunda, from Batavia! That was very elegant. But Karto was usually silent about her, although Rick loved to hear about Rose.

She was young, she wore such beautiful things, the finest jackets, pink, almost always pink, or white with pink flowers, long jackets because she was from Batavia. And an expensive brown batik kain, not a sarong, a stiff straight kain with a wide belt around her waist; and the row of gold sovereigns on her slip showed through the thin jacket. She wore rings on her fingers and heavy flat earrings, black and gold. Her hair was done in a gleaming knot—she always put some flowers in it, without the stems, white melattis or roses that Mama gave her—her hair was drawn back but not pulled tight, it waved a bit around her forehead.

"Like a dancing girl!" Urip said, and snorted angrily. Urip and Rose, they didn't mix.

In the mornings Rose put out her mat next to the sewing table where Rick and Karto were sitting now; then the second houseboy brought the sewing machine for her and put it on a little box, and then Rose sat down with her legs crossed, carefully because of the tight kain, and sewed. She sewed the dresses of Mama, and Rick's white cotton dresses with smocking and lace edging, and all the linens. She could make sheets and pillow cases with rolled hems, open seams and stitched triangles; with her supple fingers she folded the triangles and rolled the hems.

Rose lived in one of the little houses in the back of the garden, next to the laundryman; she was married to a clerk in the sugar-mill administration who got home very late every day. Her house was very neat, with plants in white-washed pots, and she kept a cockatoo. She often let the cockatoo sit on her shoulder and pick lumps of sugar from between her lips.

"Why is Urip always so angry at Rose?"

"I don't know," Karto said.

"She says that Rose is bad."

"I don't know," he repeated, and then when Rick went on asking, Karto said, "perhaps"—he always said that when he did not want to answer.

"Perhaps."

And the boy who took care of the lamps, with his wife who was the parlor maid: "Two in one family earning money, that isn't proper, that is too much!" In the evening, with the children asleep, the parlor maid gambled it away because that oaf of a husband of hers didn't dare say anything. Madam should never have hired them both.

The second houseboy was always so quiet, he never opened his mouth; he had been in jail, oh, long ago, no-body remembered—in chains—he had knifed someone. "Shhh."

"Knifed who, why?" Rick asked, but Karto didn't re-member who and why, or else he didn't want to tell.

And the first gardener, he "studied," he had to read the Koran and to fast. At times Rick and Karto could hear them in the dark silence, monotonous voices from the village repeating the same sentence over and over, in a harsh drone, and someone beating the drum in time, also harsh and monotonously. Later the gardener would go to Mecca and become a hadji with a turban on his head.

"Does that make him an Arab?" asked Rick, who was afraid of Arabs.

"Perhaps," Karto said.

But the second gardener wasn't much good, he kept bad company, with gamblers, thieves and robbers. Robbers were the worst—he would end badly! And sometimes he lured the third gardener along, who was just a boy still.

The second water carrier lay ill.

"Mark my words," Karto whispered, "that one is going to die. Several times he's found an egg with a needle, and hair, and nails, under the threshold of his house."

"What does that mean?" Rick asked, but Karto just looked around to see if anyone had overheard his words.

They came to Mangun, and Karto was silent for a moment. Mangun was number one—and good!

"And what else?" Rick asked. Karto wouldn't say more, not about Mangun, number one and an old man—that wasn't proper—but once he had told her that Mangun knew the prayers, that was why so many people came to see him, the prayer in time of sickness, misfortune, death, all the prayers.

Once, long ago, Mangun's own daughter, his only child, "and so sweet," Karto said—"she was very sick."

And for her too he had said the prayer she wanted. Rick could see her, young and sweet and all well again.

"But where is she? I've never seen her."

"She is dead," Karto said.

That frightened Rick. "And the prayer?" He had said . . .

"It was the prayer for death, don't you understand?" Karto was angry because she was so stupid.

"A man can die hard—" he curved his back as if under a burden—"but also light . . . so . . . so . . . light . . ." and his flat leathery hand made a fluttering movement upward, like a bird. Rick looked at it and nodded. She understood quite well, she thought.

But the coachman and the groom! Next to the carriage house, where the grass and the maize leaves were weighed, big rocks from the river were lying about, to be put in with the grass—and Madam never even suspected!

And then Karto got back to his mountain again.

When there was a moon, or as long as the air was clear, they could see the mountain in the night, large and dark, far and yet near, just beyond the whitewashed garden wall.

And the watchman pointed: to the left near the canyon was the old crater of the volcano which was now extinct, a holy man lived nearby, the keeper of the keys.

And to the right was the lake. Sometimes a nymph from heaven came there to bathe; before she bathed she took off her wings, they were made of feathers and shouldn't get wet. Then she bathed in the moonlight.

Until Urip got really angry and stuck her head out of

the window and cried that Rick had to come to bed immediately or else—"you better watch out!"

"You'd better go quickly," the watchman said softly, "such a big angry mouth!"

And Rick climbed back in through the window, put the latch on the blinds, and undressed. But as soon as she was in bed she went on thinking where Karto had left off; she saw the nymph bathing in the lake, her wings lying on the ground, and the wind blew, the moon shone white on the water. She shivered.

"Urip!" she called. Urip got up from her mat and put her head in through the gauze curtains. Her face was old and thin and very brown, she still held her quid in her cheek.

"He and his talk! You wait." She pulled the blue-and-white cotton blanket up, put her hand behind Rick's head, under the hair, and started rubbing with short, hard strokes.

First it hurt, then it didn't, as if a cramp had been loosened and was vanishing, and in its place something wonderfully warm and soft came up along her neck and into her head, and she forgot all the stories.

"There." Urip moved away and tucked the curtains back in under the mattress. "There, and now go to sleep, heart of mine." She said it grumpily and abruptly, because she was still angry, but it was nice to be called "heart of mine."

AND WITH THE MORNING CAME A NEW DAY.

Before it was quite light, the servants were already bathing at the two wells, buckets rattled, a block squeaked, and water was splashing fresh and cool on the stones. Karto rolled up his mat, lit a new cigarette, exchanged a few words with the other watchman under Rick's window, and left with him.

The sun rose, and the garden lay heavy with dew.

The green of the many big trees, the lawns and the bushes and the plants in bloom, wasn't yet hard and dry as it would be later in the sharp sunlight—it was soft and moist, as if everything had just budded that morning.

There was a scent of wet flowers, and Urip went to pick melattis to put in the water for washing.

Papa in long batik trousers and a starched white jacket and Mama in a silk kimono were drinking coffee on the side veranda in front of their bedroom. Rick walked in the garden; in the morning she was allowed to go barefoot. The ground was cool and soft under her feet.

The horses were groomed near the stables or taken to the river for a bath: the two blacks, the two brown ones, the two dappled ones, the two dog-cart horses for Papa, and the black one that was so nervous and not good for anything.

The little yellow cows and their calves were taken to the pasture behind the mill. Jacob, the Bengal bull, had his own pasture behind the stables. He was white and shining in the morning, with a soft skin which was too loose for him and a hump on his neck. The beautiful little son of the cowherd had liked to lie on his back and shout in his ear, and Jacob had always obeyed him.

The deer stepped carefully through the wet grass. There were chickens and turkeys, ducks and geese, rabbits and guinea pigs. There was a huge aviary with crown pigeons of a dull tender blue, so beautiful that they were bored with themselves.

In the other aviary, which had a tree, lived Jim the ape. He hunched over and picked at a branch or a stone and looked somber even on the most radiant of mornings. In the stables there was also a monkey to keep the horses company. It was always grinning, but it disapproved of the nervous horse and never went near it.

And the tame pigeons! No one knew how many there

were. They walked around on the garden paths in the early sun, colorful, fat and gleaming, following each other and bowing and roo-koo-ing.

The servants had cages near their houses with wild wood pigeons, thin little gray and brown ones. Their ways of cooing had special meanings: good luck or bad luck. Mangun knew all about these things. The white cockatoo of Rose the seamstress, with its large pink tuft, climbed around freely; it was completely tame.

In the garden there were many other birds: bright yellow weaverbirds made their nests in the palms, out on the leaves where they swayed in the wind. In the hibiscus hedges around the wells and in front of all the outbuildings, hummingbirds tumbled about, light as feathers; they hung upside down from the many flowers, inserted their long beaks, and when they flew away they made sharp little sounds. There were jalaks too, five or six together: they were rather large, shiny black birds with big beaks and harsh voices, always discussing and fighting about something. Sometimes a whole flock of chirping paddy birds came into the garden by mistake and descended on a tree or a berry bush. And the beo sat neatly in its cage and kept repeating its own name in a pleading tone—beo, beo—until Urip brought it its meal, dry rice with hot peppers, because it loved hot food.

Squirrels flew up and down the branches of the trees, lizards flitted along the roots, and an angry old gray tokèh might sit in a tree looking like a little dragon, or a chameleon with bulging eyes and a palpitating throat, and much greener than the leaves around it.

Slowly it became warmer. When her parents were through Rick had to shower—the melatti water was for her face and hands only—and get dressed. Then they had breakfast, and the day had started. The horses were hitched to the dog cart and Papa left for the cane fields.

And one day was exactly like another.

But in the afternoon, while everyone was resting, something might happen every now and again. Rick would climb out of her window, and there the two nieces Assi and Nèng would be waiting for her.

They were older than Rick, but not much, and yet they already dressed like women. Stiff slips, straight sarongs with colored belts, flowered jackets, hair done up in a knot, and pieces of rolled palm leaf in their pierced ears so that they could wear nice big earrings later. And Assi, the older, put a few flowers in her hair knot. Rick would have loved to do that too.

The garden was different now from in the morning, it lay still and languid and very green under the vibrating air; it was hot and there was no one up but the three girls. The servants were having their afternoon rest too. The animals were in stables or cages, the birds were hiding in the shade, there was only a lizard slipping away from them.

They climbed all the fruit trees and tasted all the fruits and there was no one to stop them. When the kanari nuts were ripe and falling, they sat in the cool carriage drive on the big roots and cracked the nuts between two stones. They played jacks on the veranda of the guest pavilion. Nèng cheated at times, but she was the smallest; Assi never did, she was as honest as gold.

And Assi could fold palm leaves in different shapes—a little man with legs, a woman in a sarong, a warrior's horse, a bird—that was the holy Garuda bird that protected everyone from danger. And they acted out plays.

Everywhere they had favorite spots, under some tree, on a slope beside one of the big ditches, between the ferns. With stones and water from the ditch they constructed a lake, and the palm-leaf woman was the nymph from heaven. Rick wanted to make wings for her, but Assi said no, no one was allowed to touch her little figures.

At times a complete silence fell over the garden under the trees in the sun; they stopped playing to look at each other, and they all looked around carefully to see if there wasn't a man hiding behind a tree. But there was no one.

Or Rick would play alone, she had her own tree then, a tree which belonged to her, like the old lacquered chair from Palembang. It was the second in a row of five rubber trees. They weren't high, but they had a lot of width, with thick trunks and raised roots, broad branches and large, drooping green leaves. She climbed up in it to read, or she blew on the pink bractlets of the young leaves—if you were careful you could blow them up into little longish balloons. But what she liked best was to hang over the garden wall, because below her, on the other side of the wall, was the Post Road, lined by tamarinds which were much higher than the rubber trees.

In the worst heat the road lay deserted, perhaps a single man from the village came down it hurrying home; later in the afternoon there was more traffic.

For instance, a band of traveling gamelan musicians. The racks with the gongs were carried by men, and walking behind them on the shoulder of the road came the dancing girls. Their faces were painted yellow, their hair glued to their foreheads in points, and they wore long batik kains and bodices which left the arms and shoulders bare; but on the road they covered their shoulders with beautiful long shawls.

There was something about them, Rick didn't understand what, and no one was willing to tell her.

They looked tired and dusty, but then they would suddenly laugh loudly about something and grab the ends of their shawls with their long, ringed fingers as if they were going to dance—right there on the big Post Road. But they didn't, they just walked on.

Or another procession . . .

A funeral with a covered bier and men singing.

A wedding procession, but never with the bride and groom together. Either the groom came by on a prancing horse held by his friends, or the bride in a palanquin all closed up with wooden blinds—she might be only a child, how did she look, was she beautiful?

The guests from a circumcision, and the pitiful little boy who had been circumcised huddled in someone's lap, in a ceremonial chair which was carried on long bamboos.

Or a Chinese, in his black silken trousers and black jacket, with a string of woven red silk through his pigtail. Behind him his helpers, carrying huge baskets of cotton prints and silks and embroidered cloths on their bamboo yokes. The yokes swept up and down in the rhythm of their steps, and creaked *kerret-tet-tet,* as Karto would say. The Chinese turned a little rattle between his thin fingers.

Whenever Mama bought a lot from him, he gave Rick a

flat silk doll. She glued these inside her closet doors; she already had a king, a warrior, a mandarin, a woman and a child. He was the Chinese who had lent money to Urip. Rick followed him with her eyes. She thought of Urip, who always said "heart of mine," but also of the silk dolls in her closet, and she wondered—should she hate him or not?

And when it was grinding time at the mill, the carts with the sugar cane came by in a long line, creaking and swaying on their high wooden wheels. Each cart was pulled by a team of oxen, little yellow ones, larger black-and-white or red-and-white ones, or two Bengals, as beautiful as Jacob the bull, stately and white, with bent horns, humps, loose soft skin, velvety black eyes and black nostrils.

And all, even the saddest little yellow oxen, wore bells: brass or wooden bells, large or small ones, enormous flat ones reaching to their knees. The rich Bengals sometimes had bells of silver. And those bells all rang while the animals pulled hard, the whips cracked, the teamsters shouted, the rough axles shrieked and creaked. Dust hung over the road in dense clouds.

Rick was in the shade of the foliage, the air smelled prickly and sweet with dust, cane juice, and the sweat of tired men and beasts. She watched it all silently and she became very sleepy, until a little bell startled her—a light gay bell, very different from the cow bells.

That was the confection man who came by with his little stand. That meant it was almost four o'clock, and she had to hurry back to her bedroom because four was her time to get up.

AND AS THE DAYS WERE ALL THE SAME, so were the years. The east monsoon, and then the west monsoon, and then again the east monsoon, the west monsoon.

Sunlight and dust and hot vibrating skies, hazy days, short twilights, and the long, clear tropical nights full of cool mountain wind and moon and stars. To the south the Southern Cross over the rustling trees, looking like a kite on its side, and overhead Orion, big and powerful. Delicate bamboo foliage etched against the sky; silver palm leaves washed with moonlight and waving like fans, slowly and gracefully in the night. A whispering wind.

Or violent thunderstorms, pouring rains, muddy brown rivers overflowing, a sun setting in fiery red over the steaming plain, the mountains hidden behind heavy clouds. Dark brooding nights, with a moment's breathing spell from a rattling rain. But in the morning a new world, clear and washed, with precise lines and sharp blue shadows— until the clouds gathered, the rain started falling again.

And in the stillness before that moment—from far away and yet very clear—the rainbird uttering its cries. Rick counted them.

"You mustn't listen to it!" Urip said angrily, because that brought bad luck.

The sugar cane grew in the fields and ripened, turned yellow, full of juice, and in the dry season it was cut and ground. But first came the harvest festival.

Decorated bamboo gates were set up at the entrance to the mill. Water buffalo were killed and their heads with bent horns and wide-open glassy eyes were hung near the big machines, garlands of leaves around their necks. And the buffalo blood was sprinkled on the cruel iron cylinders which crushed the sugar cane, so they would have their blood, and there needn't be any accidents. The Javanese mill workers, the teamsters and the field hands sat on their mats in long rows and ate their festival dinner. Priests led in prayer, and from time to time all the men repeated one of the long sentences.

Gamelans played day and night.

There were shows: men with horses made of bamboo gripped between their legs staged sham battles. The horses had high, curved necks, real manes and tails, and were decorated with garlands of flowers; the men made them prance and neigh, and they fought each other with wooden sabers.

And there were shows with shadow puppets: the black shadows of the fine leather puppets moved on a white screen. Before the show began a leather triangle was set up in front of the screen. It was artfully cut, in all colors, and on each side was a snake with gaping jaws. It symbolized the world—the setting for the play.

There were dancers in gaudy costumes, with stiff faces painted yellow, or wearing wooden masks.

In the big house cooks from the town were at work preparing a banquet; there was a tremendous commotion. After the dinner a ball was held in the godown of the mill, complete with dance programs that had silken tassels and little pencils attached. But Rick didn't care too much about all this, for she wasn't allowed to stay up—either for the dinner or for the ball.

When the festival was all over, and before the rains, there came the nicest time of the year. There were always guests in the house then, or Rick and her parents went to stay with other people. Not often and not for long, because Papa did not like it and he didn't like to be alone for long either. But they did go to see Aunt Nancy, and every year between monsoons they went to the mountains, to the old gentleman.

Aunt Nancy was a cousin of Papa and of Uncle Fred, Papa's youngest brother. When they were children, they had all lived in the same village in Holland, near the sea; now she lived here, at the Chinese mill.

It was a sugar mill, but it had once belonged to a Chinese and everything about it looked different. The house had a roof with curled-up edges and there were pierced glazed tiles, green or brown, set into the outer walls. These might be in the shape of a letter or a figure or an animal, and through the open spaces you could see the green of the trees, a piece of sky, or in the evening suddenly a star. They let air in too, for there weren't many windows. All the woodwork, including the beams of the ceiling, had been lacquered a reddish brown. Aunt Nancy said that she liked that.

Things were arranged differently from at home too. Aunt Nancy did not like whitewashed flower pots on stands, silk screens against the draft, and lace-edged portieres with draped valances. She had colored linen curtains and a few old-fashioned paper screens for the open doorways. There were little faded figures on the screens, people walking in the mountains or rowing on lakes between fantastic rocks and trees. Everywhere in the house there were plants with leaves of all colors, plants that other people would put in their gardens. They stood in green or yellow glazed pots, right on the floor, on the fine matting, because there was no marble.

It was not a big house; the outbuildings were much larger. Perhaps the Chinese family had lived in them. They formed a whole row of high, hollow rooms without ceilings, with stone floors, white walls, and smoke-blackened beams under a tile roof. They had air holes and huge tarred doors which were opened and closed with wooden levers. In one of those unused rooms a Chinese lantern almost as tall as a man was hanging from the beams, old banners and wooden standards lacquered red and gold were standing against the blind walls. And on the floor lay a discarded dragon which had once been carried by twenty or thirty men in the Chinese New Year processions, with a light burning in its head.

Whenever Rick begged her to, Aunt Nancy would light a candle in the lantern and close the heavy door. Then the soft, golden light shone through the dark on the threatening and melancholy head of the old Dragon of Happiness.

And Aunt Nancy also had a porcelain tea pavilion.

At the back of the garden there was an orchard of Savu trees—neat little trees in stiff rows, looking as if they had been pruned with scissors—and precisely in the middle of the orchard was a round tiled pond, and in the middle of the pond, across a little arched bridge, stood a kiosk with a green roof. The green tiled roof rested on six little pillars and had curled-up edges decorated with flowers of green, blue and yellow porcelain, and porcelain bells. There was an openwork railing over the water, where lotus leaves floated on long stems.

No one had ever seen such a tea pavilion, so funny, so prissy, so green. Aunt Nancy said, "You mustn't mind, I'm still jealous of your marble floor."

Her husband, Uncle Rudolf, was much older than she and terribly serious, he always worked late in the laboratory of the factory, he was making an invention. When he came home, Rick saw how he always stared at Aunt Nancy. But who wouldn't stare at Aunt Nancy?

Mama was well dressed, and she looked sweet with her

beautiful brown eyes and her curly forelock—in the morning, in her blue or pink sarong from Pekalongan with its lace-trimmed jacket, velvet pumps with paillettes and high heels; in the afternoon, in a white dress with stiff embroidery, and when she went out, in a silk with puffed sleeves and a big bow in the back. But not like Aunt Nancy—no.

"Nancy is elegant," Papa once said. Elegant was different from just neat, it was something special, it had something to do with clothes but not very much.

Aunt Nancy wore a long dress in the morning—called a bébé—instead of a sarong and jacket. But her bébés weren't of starched white cotton with embroidery. She liked neither cotton nor embroidery, and least of all starch. Her bébés were made of nainsook or of thin batiste. Almost everyone wore black stockings, but she wore light ones, with shoes to match her dress. And in the evening, if there was a party, a lace or tulle dress hovered like a cloud around her.

Her eyes were a very light transparent blue, clear, with a dark circle and the center dark too; her blond hair was put up high over her straight white neck. For a while she had had bangs, very fair and gleaming; she kept jumping up to go comb them somewhere behind a door. When she came back, she would tilt her head and ask, "Is it proper now?" and everyone said that it was proper.

And she was gay, which most people weren't, but at the same time she was so restless, always fluttering around without knowing what she wanted. She liked to dress up and act out some role. Rick could join in, there was a trunkful of costumes.

Aunt Nancy might play an old lady, in a heavy black

dress with a black-and-white boa of ostrich feathers, a bonnet with ribbons and purple violets—pensées, they were called, she said. And Rick had white pantaloons to put on, a wide skirt, shoes with velvet laces that criss-crossed up her legs, and her hair parted in the middle with curls over each ear.

"And remember to call me Granny," Aunt Nancy said.

Rick's favorite role was as a Chinese. She wore a purple jacket with a gold dragon in front and in the back. It was much too big, and Aunt Nancy pinned the sleeves up and put a wide Italian sash around her waist. It didn't belong, but it looked fine, Rick thought, and she also wore a gold net over her hair. Aunt Nancy wore a black skirt and a black brocade jacket stiff with gold embroidery. There was a high red stool onto which she climbed; she was the Empress and Rick brought her a basket of fruit, bowing down to the floor. But Aunt Nancy didn't look at her, she sat frozen on the red lacquered stool, her head bent, and she traced the pattern on her jacket with her finger.

"The waves of the sea," she said thoughtfully. But then she looked up.

"I could very well be a Chinese woman, Riquette, and you my Chinese daughter." She always called Rick "Riquette."

Once Mama had received a letter from Uncle Fred with a note in it, all folded up, for Nancy.

"Thank you," Aunt Nancy had said, and put the note in her belt.

"Don't you want to see what Fred has to say?" Mama asked.

"Oh yes, later!" Aunt Nancy said. "I have no time now,

I still have some cooking to do." And she ran to the kitchen to make a pudding, a mushroom pudding with burnt sugar, that was a complicated recipe; usually the cook did it.

Later Rick couldn't find her anywhere, either in the house or in the garden. When she came to the dragon room, the door was closed; she lifted the latch and peeked in. The yellow lantern was burning, Aunt Nancy was standing under it in the yellow glow. She wore a white dress, she held a little white note in her hand, and she was nodding smilingly, nodding "yes" to someone in the distance. The dying dragon at her feet looked up at her with his bulging black eyes.

When she saw Rick, she became very angry.

"When you want to come into a room and the door is closed, you must knock, Rick." It sounded so severe, and "Rick"—she never said that.

But the following day she had forgiven Rick and she took her to the tea pavilion with a book and candies. She read to her, stories of knights, of the inn in the Spessart mountains, and the fairy tales of Andersen. And when she read about the little mermaid, she became very sad and closed the book.

Rick was sad about it too, that it ended so badly. Sad things could happen in a story, that was all right, because everything might still turn out well. But a sad ending, that was terrible, that couldn't be changed, it was forever.

OR Aunt Nancy came to stay
with them, in the big house. And when Uncle Fred came
too, Aunt Nancy said, "now we're children again, all together," and looked from Uncle Fred to Papa. And then
the three of them were probably thinking of the village
with the linden trees and the stone pump in the square in
front of the church, and Sunday school, and all the people
at home, and the North Sea.

Uncle Fred was Papa's youngest brother, a half-brother,
and not yet married. He was an officer, cavalry, that was
very elegant. Aunt Nancy called him Daddy longlegs, and
Papa said mockingly, "milord," because he always came

with such an entourage, his own horse and a groom, one or two saddles, all his trunks, and Buyung.

Uncle Fred didn't look very much like Papa because he had no goatee and he was blond. But he was tall and thin, very thin—a cavalry man has to be—his face seemed especially thin with its sunken temples, and he often pressed his lips together, which made hollows in his cheeks. This didn't make him look old but on the contrary boyishly fragile and a bit peaked. His sharp gray eyes lay deep in their sockets and he often stared into the distance; then Aunt Nancy would snap her fingers. And he could suddenly start laughing too, like Papa, but different again, for he was really gay about something; he always bent over when he laughed like that, with his hand on his stomach as if he had a pain—but he didn't.

And Buyung was his servant, his orderly.

He was no Javanese but a Batak, from Sumatra. He looked different from the Javanese; he was heavily built, short and thick-set and very ugly—dark, almost black— with a flat nose and a wide jaw that jutted out. He walked like a sailor, with a strange swaying tread, his shoulders rocking and his overlong arms dangling. He had indeed been at sea for a long time, ferrying horses from the outlying islands. He had been everywhere.

But if anyone asked Uncle Fred where he had found Buyung, he laughed and said, "Oh, once upon a time, in the jungle, on Sumatra."

Buyung was always messily dressed in short dark trousers and a jacket, or only the trousers with a wide belt and his big knife stuck in it. On his head he wore a kerchief, bound haphazardly without nice folds, but two points always stuck out from behind one ear in a dashing way.

And he behaved differently too, he didn't care about what was proper and not proper; he talked and laughed loudly with a wide-open mouth full of chewing tobacco which would almost fall out.

All day long he followed Uncle Fred around, cleaned his room, laid out his clothes, quarreled with the laundry-man or a maid about the laundry, and saw to it that the horse was well taken care of. For Uncle Fred was terribly precise about his horse. It had to be curry-combed, bathed, dried, rubbed down, walked with its cannons bound, or exercised in the big pasture behind the stables. Buyung made fences for jumping and Uncle Fred practiced taking them. No one was allowed to watch closely except Buyung.

And Uncle Fred would rein in his horse and call Buyung over. He sat straight and slender in his white suit on the beautiful glossy horse, then he bent down a little, the reins in one hand and his riding crop in the other. Buyung stood like a rock beside him and lifted up his dark face, he said solemnly "yes, sir," "certainly," or "no, sir"; he knew a lot about horses and riding and jumping. But then suddenly they would start laughing about something together. Buyung shouted Allah's holy name a few times in his thundering voice, and smacked himself so loudly on his fat thigh that the horse pulled its head away nervously.

"Calm down, sweetheart!" Uncle Fred said and stroked

the horse gently, sat up straight in the saddle again and
rode off for some more jumping. Buyung stood nearby
and watched.

In those days it was always gay in the house, and Uncle
Fred thought up all kinds of things to do.

They had picnics on the big boulders near the river, under the bamboo trees.

Or they drove out to an old Chinese tomb in the hills,
which had a tiled platform and two red stone lions on
columns. The lions were there to guard the dead of long
ago. From the platform they could see the mill with its
chimneys and all the houses, also the big house, white in
its green garden.

And in the evenings there were often more guests, for
cards and for dancing. Then the huge round couch was put
out on the front veranda, right on top of the black marble
star. It was an ottoman, covered in flowered damask, with a
heavy stand in the center on which a bronze Flora was
holding up a cornucopia. Mama put long branches of
greens and orchids in it. And the ladies sat on the ottoman
in a circle, their backs toward one another, and the gentlemen approached, bowed, and invited them to dance.
Someone played the piano, waltzes usually, sometimes a
polka, and if there were many people a Dashing White
Sergeant or a quadrille.

Scrapings of wax candles had been strewn on the floor,
and the dancing made it as smooth as ice. It didn't shine as
much as usual, but it did mirror vaguely all those dancing
feet, fragments of white trouser legs and the colored edges
of dresses. Once in a great while Rick was allowed to dance,

Aunt Nancy practiced with her in the morning—one-two-three—but she wasn't very good at it and waltzing made her dizzy.

She loved to watch, though: the round ottoman, Flora with her flowers, the couples. Mama danced a bit stiffly, but very controlled; she never tired. Papa was a good dancer. But Uncle Fred was the best of all; he danced with long supple steps and he could waltz in both directions. He danced a lot with Aunt Nancy; at times he would almost let go of her, just holding her by the hands and pulling her in a wide circle, then back again toward him—her long skirt fluttered around her quick, narrow feet. And it was as if she flew around him and then back into his arms.

In the closed back gallery the sewing table with its extensions was laid for supper: a white damask cloth, and lots of silver, china and crystal. In the center was an oval-shaped mirror with glass trays on it holding pink roses and maidenhair fern. There were glass chains between the trays, as if they were flower ships at anchor, reflected in the water.

The days flew by. "It's feast time," the servants said; and even the grumpy old cook tried to do her best. On the landing in front of the kitchen stood an iron box on little legs, in which a cake was baked every day. There was charcoal underneath and on top, and the nieces Assi and Nèng took turns squatting next to it and fanning the embers. When the confection man came, Uncle Fred distributed cookies. Everyone was content.

Except Urip. She didn't want to take a hand in anything, she didn't laugh about anything, she wore her oldest and most threadbare jacket, and her hair hung loose. She looked ill.

That was because of Buyung!

As soon as she was alone with Rick in her room, to help her with her clothes or to brush her hair, she started talking about it.

"Heart of mine, you must listen—you mustn't have anything to do with him. A Batak! From Sumatra! He is different—really, really—he is a cannibal!" and whispering mysteriously: "He has different spit. You must listen!"

Rick didn't want to listen at all when Urip maligned Buyung. But once she had gone to ask Uncle Fred whether Buyung was really a cannibal. After all, it was possible.

Uncle Fred knew about the feud between those two, and said, "Is that what your angel Urip told you?" But Rick didn't answer that.

"Come with me!" And he took her by the hand as if she were a little child, and walked with her through the garden to the stables.

"Buyung, Buyung, where is Buyung?" he called.

Buyung was preparing the horse's feed, but he immediately came running, his big knife in his hand. He must have been chopping grass with it, little pieces of grass were stuck all along the edge.

"What is it, sir, is something wrong?" he asked.

"Do you ever eat human flesh, Buyung?" Uncle Fred asked quite casually, as if it were the most normal thing in the world.

Buyung just stared at him at first. "But certainly, sir," he then said.

"How is that done? My niece here would like to know."

Buyung stared again. "With a knife, sir," he answered, and with a strangely adroit yet very careful movement he pulled his knife along his lips, from the left corner of his mouth to the right, while turning his head against it; then he did the same in the opposite direction, from right to left—he was drinking the blood off it. He spit the pieces of grass on the ground.

"You like human flesh?"

"Yes, sir, I do."

"Would you have some now, if I invited you to?"

"Certainly, sir."

"Well, Rick, you've heard—are you satisfied?"

But then he said something in an undertone to Buyung —she could hear only the word "Urip"—and they both started to giggle like children.

What manners! Rick tried to laugh too, she didn't quite know what to think of it—was it true or wasn't it? She would not forget the way Buyung had licked his knife.

And then they had all left again, Uncle Fred, Buyung, the horse and the groom. Uncle Rudolf had come to get Aunt Nancy.

Urip revived, she oiled and combed her hair and put on a clean jacket.

"In the afternoon, during the rest hour, I'll make a treat for you," she promised Rick and the two nieces.

Rick hesitated.

"Oh, all right," she then said, distantly, as adults sometimes do.

The marble floor was mopped with hot soapy water and polished, and it spread out again like a clear lake. It was quiet in the house, very quiet and dull, nothing happened.

But within herself Rick hid something she couldn't tell anyone.

On the Sunday morning of the picnic in the hills near the Chinese tomb—most of the guests were already back in the carriages which had been waiting at the foot of the hill; the tablecloth, the knives and forks and dishes had been packed. The dog cart in which Uncle Fred and Aunt Nancy had come was still standing empty. Then Rick had walked back to look for a handkerchief someone had lost; she had climbed back up the steep path, looked around the tomb, there was no handkerchief in sight. And then suddenly she saw two people standing between the trees in the little wood behind one of the red lions. They were Uncle Fred and Aunt Nancy. They didn't see her. Uncle Fred stood with his back to Rick, Aunt Nancy had her arms around his neck, her cheek pressed against his, her eyes were closed and she kept saying, "No, Fred—no, Fred—no, no, no."

Rick had turned around and run back to the carriage as fast as she could. Why did Aunt Nancy say no? She shouldn't say no to Uncle Fred.

AND A LITTLE LATER IN THE YEAR, in the terrible heat before the rains came, Rick and her mother went on a visit to the old gentleman who lived up in the mountains. It was far; the trip took two days and Papa didn't come along. Urip did come—that was the proper way to go visiting.

Urip would look very dignified, in a batik sarong stiff with newness, a flowered jacket, and slippers. "Against the cold," she said self-consciously. She had powdered her face and done her hair neatly. She had got her rings and earrings out of pawn, and she wore a batik stole around her shoulders with pockets in which she carried things for the trip, parcels of food and a brass box with sirih and chewing tobacco. And in one hand she held a real silver spittoon. Rick couldn't take her eyes off her.

She and Mama wore gray linen travel costumes with long sleeves, and black shoes and stockings. Mama had a blue veil hanging down from her hat. They took two iron trunks painted yellow, a basket of food, Mama's black leather toilet case with its silver-topped flasks, and Urip's mat, neatly bound up with her pillow and blanket and clothes in it.

First they drove to town, to the railroad station, and then they got on the train; to go somewhere by train was quite a thing. Urip traveled third-class, Mama and Rick first-class.

There were green screens on the windows to let the air in and keep out the big cinders from the engine; they made the world outside look odd and different and even greener than it was already. The fine coal dust turned everyone black all the same.

Mama first looked among the passengers for acquaintances—if she found any, she would laugh and talk with them. Otherwise she sat very erect, looked through the screen and kept pointing out things, "Look there, Rick!" as if Rick didn't see it herself. And she whispered, "Don't stare at other people, Rick."

After a few hours they got off to change trains, and late in the afternoon they came to a big town and slept that night in a hotel. The following morning there was a stage-coach waiting for them.

A real stagecoach!

It had four horses, little skinny ones, but still four. A coachman in the box, and then two runners who stood on a board at the back like footmen. But when the road became steep they jumped off and walked beside the horses, cracked their short whips, clacked with their tongues, made a *rrrt* sound, like a drum, and just shouted. Sometimes they took hold of the bridles of the front horses and pulled them along. When the road evened out again, they jumped back on to rest, but for a long time their breath came heavily and in jerks.

Somewhere along the way they stopped to change horses. Mama and Rick stayed in the coach and ate from their basket. At the side of the road under the high tamarinds was a little shop; the coachmen and the runners, the men who had brought the fresh horses and Urip in her slippers, all stood around and drank coffee. Afterward the men squatted and smoked and talked, but Urip climbed back into the coach—she sat facing Rick and Mama on the little bench—and when she sat down she said, "Excuse me, Madam." That was the proper way.

Suddenly a whole flock of children appeared at the shop, staring at them. One put out his hand and asked for candy money.

Urip became angry. "Don't bother the lady and the miss," she scolded.

But Mama said, "Oh, the poor creatures, Urip," and gave them some pennies.

And the coach drove on again. It was a long and steep road. It became cold, the new horses went slowly, they were getting tired and there was foam on their flanks. On the short, flat stretches the breathing of the runners sounded like the squeaking of a saw.

Then they came to the mountain pass, finally!

They stopped and the horses were unhitched, for now the coach was going to be pulled by water buffaloes on a wooden yoke. The buffaloes were nervous and they snorted and tried to butt at the horses, but the men held them and harnessed them to the coach with ropes. They weren't big, but solid and strong and gray. They walked a little sideways under the yoke because of their large horns, the left horn of one and the right horn of the other crossed. The coachman stayed on the box although there were no reins to hold, the men led the buffaloes, straightened the yoke constantly, shouted and cracked whips. They went very slowly, at a walking pace. On the left was a ravine, with scarlet orchids growing in the grass and a hedge of wild roses around a sloping field. A brook ran somewhere. A high wind was blowing coldly and bleakly.

At the top the buffaloes were unhitched—they had been needed for the steep ascent only—and the coach went on with the horses. But soon afterward it stopped and they got out. They walked down a side road until they came to a little white house in a garden. The men carried the luggage.

In front of the house under a crooked old tree stood a stone statue of a seated elephant. To the side was a little lane with mulberry trees. Here the old gentleman lived on his land.

"A toy land!" Papa said, but he didn't like the old gentleman.

The house was built of bamboo and wood, and it stood on poles like a large native house—but everything was well painted. There was just one main room, with a big window, a few bedrooms, and outbuildings in back. The floors everywhere creaked. The old gentleman had only two servants, an old cook who also cleaned the house, and a boy for the garden. He himself took care of the flowers; there were flowers everywhere, and all around the house a wide border of heliotrope grew, filling the rooms with its heavy, sweet perfume.

In the front garden there wasn't much besides the crooked tree with the statue and a low wall of crumbling gray stone which ran along the side of the road. The road lay low between two steep shoulders which were covered with trees, a kind of pine with curving branches and long gray-green needles that rustled in the wind. It was such a strange road, so narrow and deep-set under the gray trees, so still and abandoned; rarely did anyone come along it. Who would have come along it?

At the back of the house, seen through the big window, was a whole world. Directly behind the house lay a ravine, a wide, deep ravine full of ferns, and farther on a wood, and green mountain ridges everywhere. But beyond all that—far away and deep down—lay the plain, light yellow, hazy and sunny. And from that plain, quite abruptly, rose two mountains, one next to the other. During the day they sometimes vanished in the misty, warm air; but later in the afternoon when it cleared, there they were again: slate-colored or blue or scarlet, together, rising from the plain—the twins of the old gentleman.

There was something about him, Rick had never known what. He was a relative of Mama's, yet not quite; he had been married to Mama's mother for a short time—she had been dead many years now—but he wasn't Mama's father. Mama always addressed him as "sir" and when she talked about him she called him "the old gentleman" as everyone else did. He wasn't really that old, but very thin and yellow; Mama said that he had a disease and often much pain. He smelled of a strong medicine, tar-like.

He had thin dark hair, white at the sides, and running from his nose along his mouth down to his chin were two deep lines, as if someone had engraved them there.

He was very clever, he could speak all three kinds of Javanese—high, middle and low—and he knew everything about plants and herbs, as well as the history and the stories of long ago of the Hindu Empire. "The old Empire," he called it.

"And he also knows witchcraft," Papa said. That was something about a calendar. "The day to marry, or to die, or to have a child, or to go stealing without getting caught," Papa said, "isn't that it, Anna?" But Mama didn't answer, she didn't like it when Papa talked that way.

Once the old gentleman himself had begun talking about his witchcraft. The three of them were sitting around the table at the big windows. It was late in the afternoon. The sun was still shining, but from the plains thin shreds of mist began to climb up the mountains. First they sank into the dark-blue ravines, then they slowly rose and covered the purple slopes like a blanket.

Mama had poured the tea, there were cakes, and they

were sitting there very cozily. Then the old gentleman got up, opened a drawer and took out a little velvet bundle.

"I'm going to show you something!" He spread the piece of velvet out on the table; there were three rings on it, two gold rings with stones, one of plain gold. He took the rings one by one, held them up, said their names, and put them down again.

"The elephant" was a kind of signet ring, but very large, with a green stone—oblong and transparent—in which an elephant was carved.

"Nandi the bull" was the small figure—unbelievably small—of a gold bull set in a gold ring.

"The crabs" was the most beautiful. Two crabs holding each other; two round white stones formed their shells, and all the legs and claws were carved from fine gold, very, very delicately.

The rings were lying next to each other on the velvet, and Rick bent over and touched them one by one with her finger, the elephant, the bull, the crabs. "Is it a treasure?" she asked.

"Careful!" Mama said.

But the old gentleman told her, "It's all right. Yes, that's a treasure," and after a moment, "from the old Empire."

The rings remained on the table, and Mama passed the cakes, and then she suddenly asked, had the rings been found here? Had people come to the house to sell them?

The old gentleman hesitated. "Yes, they were found here," he then said. "The Javanese don't like that kind of thing in their houses, they are simple peasants. The rings are so old, they know that, and often with animals . . .

You never know about animals, are they malevolent or good? They wouldn't sell them to strangers, but me they know well, and so they bring those things here. And I give them money, or whatever else they want. They know I won't cheat them. And often I can give them something else in the bargain. Yes, Anna—" he laughed a bit ironically— "you know, I can tell the good and the bad days."

"But . . . but you don't believe in that yourself, do you?" Mama asked.

"Oh, yes," he said. "I can't quite explain it in a few words. It has mainly to do with combinations of the names of the days, the days of the five-day week and the days of the seven-day week."

"Like Friday the thirteenth being a bad day to go on a trip?" Mama asked.

The old gentleman laughed again. "Yes," he said, "but this goes further. The names of the people come into it too; and the sky, and North, South, East and West, each with its good and evil spirits. And then there is the direction of the Snake. That is rather complicated, because it changes, and one must never go against the direction of the Snake—except in battle. And there are numbers too, a lot of numbers! It sounds involved, but it isn't really. It isn't new but old and tried, I'd say, passed on from generation to generation."

"Do you mean to say that it works?" Mama asked.

"Oh, yes," he said again, "but you have to believe in it, it's always that way. I didn't make it up, I only had to write it down and now I can pass it on."

"It must be wonderful to help people!" Mama said. Her voice sounded so odd.

But then the old gentleman shook his head. "No, no," he said. "Do understand, Anna, I'm not saying that I can help. I only know the day."

He pushed his chair away from the table and rested his head against its high back. He looked so ill, more yellow than ever, the black and white hair so thin, the lines around the nose and mouth so deep. Mama didn't say anything more either.

That was the only time that the witchcraft was mentioned.

THE DAYS ON THE TOY LAND of the old gentleman flew by.

In the mornings Rick and her mother went on walks in the mountains, through the green and the coolness and all the different kinds of flowers; the sound of water was everywhere. Or they sat in the garden, in the lane under the mulberry trees. Or Mama made something in the kitchen, together with Urip and the old cook. She had brought along a thick cookbook full of handwritten recipes.

Mama was different here from the way she was at home. She was much gayer and younger, and she talked a lot about all sorts of things. Rick thought at times that here she loved Mama as much as Aunt Nancy. After lunch Mama rested, but Rick could play in the garden; she climbed one of the mulberry trees, her mouth and hands got purple with mulberries—sweet, sweet, sweet—and she sat on the roots of the crooked tree and watched the statue.

"Ganeesha, he with the elephant's head," the old gentleman said. For the statue wasn't a real elephant, it had a human body with arms and legs, four arms; it was seated with its feet together on a pillow of lotus. Often flowers were placed at its feet—white melattis or light-green tjempakkas, and a bit of yellow wax, some ashes of incense. People still sacrificed to it, in the dark so that no one would see.

Or Rick would go with Urip and the old cook to bathe and wash their hair in the spring near the village. Urip had taken off her rings and earrings, but she still wore her slippers and her pink flannel jacket. The cook went barefoot, in an old sarong and a faded blue bodice, but she was only "one from the mountains." Urip and the cook each carried a bowl; in one was the blackish water drawn from burned rice leaves, in the other clean water with roses and melatti buds for rinsing. They had to walk slowly because of the bowls and because of Urip's slippers. On the way the two old women quarreled. The cook said that so many people always came to the old gentleman, from far away, from the mountains, from the Dièng, even from beyond the Dièng!

"Oh . . . well, where are they? I don't see them," Urip said.

"No, of course not, when there are guests they're too shy to come!" Yes of course they were shy, those "mountain people," because of the lady and the miss and Urip.

"Why do they come?" Urip inquired in a superior tone of voice.

"To ask for help," the cook said.

"What kind of help?"

"Help . . . the old gentleman is very wise!"

"Oh, wise! Is he perhaps a 'rich one'?"

No, the cook had to admit that he wasn't a "rich one," "but he is wise all the same!"

"Oh," Urip said, and shrugged and was silent; it was impossible to talk to these mountain people.

They passed the little village, just a few houses behind green hedges in the afternoon sun. A narrow, steep side path, a small ravine, and there in the shade of many trees was the spring.

A stone cistern must have stood there once, but three of its walls had collapsed and only the back wall still stood, propped up by the slope behind it on which the trees grew. Their roots reached down through the blocks of stone and held them as if in a rope net. Two yellow bamboo pipes projected from the broken wall, and from them spurts of limpid water splashed on the worn stone floor.

On the slope, but back in among the trees, covered by shadows and low-hanging leaves, another statue stood. This one was older than old, the gray stone was weathered and chipped, eroded by moisture, covered with fungus and heavy green moss.

Who was it? Was it the god Shiva, dancing? He was

standing on one leg, bent at the knee, the other leg lifted, a fringed sash around the waist, the upper part of the body leaning over, the broken-off arms stretched upward alongside the tilted head which was crowned with a high tiara—dancing the dance of destruction. They undressed behind the trees. Urip gave Rick one of her sarongs to put on, high under the arms and knotted tight the way the two old women did theirs. Under the water spouts naked children from the village were jumping about, and Urip chased them away: "Can't you see that the lady wants to bathe?" The children walked away, then stood still and stared at them.

First Rick bathed with Urip and the cook under the crystal cold water. After that she had to sit on a stone, her eyes closed and her head back, while Urip washed her hair with the sharp, smoky water from the rice straw, with water from the spring, and finally with the flower water. Then she wound a dry towel around her hair—she could go back under the spout again, "but watch that you don't wet your head, heart of mine!"

They dressed behind the trees, Urip made herself a new quid, put on her slippers, and they went back home with the wet sarongs in the bowls. The village children were jumping around in the water again.

And on the moist green spot between the trees the statue remained, one leg gracefully lifted, sash flying, lost within itself.

Then they had tea at the round table near the window, with the old gentleman. They had dinner there too, after dark, with the lamp burning. Sometimes the old gentleman told a story, of gods and goddesses, of Ganeesha in the front garden, how he had got his elephant's head and his one broken tusk. Ganeesha had broken off the tusk himself and thrown it into the sky and now it was the moon—the ivory half-moon. He had aimed it at the sun, who was mocking him.

"The Lord Sun and his twenty-eight starry wives," the old gentleman said. He told of the brothers Rama and Laksmana, and the princess Sita—the story sculptured on the Prambanan temples. And he told of the Burubudur, the huge temple with the seven terraces of which one had been buried by sand.

And of Buddha.

And then Rick had to go to bed. She listened to their voices for a long time, and then Mama came to sleep with her in the same bed in the guest room, and Urip slept in the room too, on her mat under a blanket.

Outside, down in the village, there was a bronze gong hanging from a tree—a gong from the old Empire. Every time the night watchman passed, he sounded it. It was a very different sound from the tong-tong of the plains, not so dark and threatening, but clear and simple in the cool mountain air. And every time the watchman called out some words, ending on a high note as if quoting a line from a poem.

And then their visit was almost over. On the last day, in the afternoon, Mama had gone in to make the tea and Rick was standing in front of the house with the old gentleman. He was leaning against the garden wall—when he was on his feet he always leaned against something—and he looked down the road which was lying quietly and wearily under the sun and the shadow.

"Shall I tell you about the road?" he asked. "It's an old road. I know that there's another one, and some people say that that was the road, but no, this was the road! Centuries ago, then as now—this same road. And he with the elephant's head—" he pointed at the statue in the garden — "and also the other statue at the spring, which is Shiva, were already standing here. All along the road were little temples and statues. So many stones from them have been found, people have used them for everything, for this garden wall too." He put his hand on it. "Such a pity!

"But high up on the plain, on the Dièng, was a city of temples and monasteries only, a holy city. And the people from the plain went up this way on pilgrimages; it was a long way and at the end they had to climb the high steps in the mountainside, then as now.

"Once a year the King passed by—there was a king then —he went to the holy city to fast and to pray as a good king should. Priests and monks came down to meet him, perhaps down to here, making much noise with bronze gongs and drums and blowing on shells.

"Have you ever heard a shell horn?"

"No," Rick said, "no."

"No," the old gentleman said, "nor I, but I feel that I can quite imagine how it was." And he went on, "All those bright banners and flags fluttering in the wind!" He moved his hand back and forth as he said that; a gust of wind blew over the road and threw up some dust and made the pines rustle. There was no one on the road.

"The holy city has crumbled into ruins," the old gentle-man said sadly. And later, when they were walking back to the house along the mulberry lane, he added, "There are some ruins up there of little stone temples, the others must have been built of wood. But it is beautiful there, as beautiful as it was then. We should have gone once, the three of us, along the old road, not the new one, and up the mountain stairs; I could have led the way."

"But let's do it next year," Rick said immediately; she loved going places. "Yes, can we, and on horses?" she asked enthusiastically.

The old gentleman laughed softly. "I don't know that I can go the the Dièng next year, Rick, and then—on a horse! I'm terribly sorry." His voice was low but odd, very emphatic. It startled Rick.

What did he mean? Did he mean that he . . . ? She gave him such a frightened look that he noticed it; he stopped and touched her with his hand as if to reassure her.

"You mustn't mind," he said. "I don't." Nothing more; and he didn't look depressed or sad, just old and thin and yellow, as always.

"Come along now, Anna will be waiting for us with the tea"; when he spoke of Mama he called her Anna. But he was rather silent that last evening.

And the following morning the men from the coach came for the luggage. The old cook and the gardener wished them "a happy voyage," Mama gave them some money from her purse and wished them happiness too. Urip was wearing her best things again. They walked through the garden, along the road, and to the main road where the coach was waiting; they said goodbye to the old gentleman, got in and drove off. When they turned to wave, they saw him standing there, leaning on his cane; he looked after them for a long time but he soon stopped waving.

"The old gentleman is getting old," Mama said with pity in her voice.

But the next day, on the train, she had changed already. She kept looking at her watch, which was fastened to her dress with a gold pin. Suppose the train was late and they would miss their connection! Papa would have to wait!

Rick asked, "We are going again next year, aren't we, and can we go to the Dièng then?"

Mama answered, "Oh, yes, if Papa gives his permission."

Rick fell silent and looked out through the green screen; she had a headache from the heat of the plains. She didn't long for home at all.

And shortly afterward the old gentleman died.

Mama was crying when she told Rick, and Rick started to cry too.

"Now we won't go to the Dièng," Rick sobbed.

"Oh, for shame," Mama said. "Is that what you are crying about? The Dièng! What does the Dièng matter, it's the old gentleman. I thought you loved him too."

Rick did not answer; of course she loved him, she cried for him, for everything together.

Because the old gentleman was not only himself. He was also the garden with the heliotrope and the mulberry trees, the twin mountains, "he with the elephant's head" and Shiva at the spring, the good-luck days, and the holy city on the Dièng which had crumbled into dust—and now all that was gone. How could Mama not understand?

Later one of the rings came, the most beautiful one, the ring with the crabs: Mama had inherited it. She put it in her red velvet jewel box, it was too big to wear, but she let Rick look at it whenever she straightened her closets.

Rick had inherited a woman's creese, a little dagger, in a silver sheath. Mama kept it for her.

"We'll have a paper knife made of it for you later," she said.

THAT WAS THE FACE OF LIFE for Rick in those days, the face of people, animals and things around her. But there was also, hidden, the other side. The other side of goodness: evil; of light, darkness; of life, death.

And when she met it, she became afraid, for she was a fearful child by nature.

Some time earlier there had been another family at the mill with children her age; they were gone now. There had been a boy a bit older than she who was her playmate, and a smaller sister who was made to play at being their child but who never wanted to do what they told her.

59

Rick had often gone to their house, even after dinner in the evening.

At eight o'clock precisely Mangun would come to get her with the lantern, and they would walk back to Rick's house in the dark. First through the strange garden, across the little bridge, and then along the Post Road. As long as they could see her, the two children called after her, "Goodbye! Bye!" but then they would suddenly and completely forget her.

On the Post Road it was pitch-dark under the trees, and silent.

Mangun would take her hand, and with the other he held up the lantern to throw the light in front of their feet. (She was bigger now; it wouldn't be the thing any more for him to hold her by the hand, but it was all right then.) His hand was always cold, not clammy, but dry and cool, with hard fingers; that was because he was so old. They walked slowly, sometimes they met others, little groups of people, one man carrying a torch or a bottle of oil with a burning wick in it.

These were flickering, restless lights, and their bearers swung them back and forth, making the lights flicker even more. Monstrous shadows fell on the road and against the tree trunks and upward against the heavy foliage above their heads. Everything seemed distorted and wrong. Faces couldn't be seen properly; they were strange, dark shapes with holes for eyes, looking at Rick and Mangun.

It was very quiet; there was only the shuffling of bare feet. When people passed each other, they had to slow down in order to exchange proper greetings; that took a moment. There were always the questions: "Where are you from?" and "Where are you going?" and always the answers—from and to, the North or the South or the East or the West. Seldom more than that. Rick didn't know why that frightened her so. These strangers, in the dark, and the way they said the North, the South, the East, the West —as if they were creatures frozen at those four points.

How could they come from there or go there? Who or what and where? It might very well be nothing and nobody and nowhere.

Rick held on hard to Mangun's hand and she never said anything when they passed others, but Mangun always answered quietly the "where from?" and "where to?": "from the big house" and "to the big house."

He didn't go down one of the long carriage drives with her, but the back way, along the white, dusty field where the pressed cane stalks were dried, and through the little gate in the wall at the back of the garden. Then they were immediately in the lit-up outbuildings, the big kitchen which was always open, where the cook was working with the two nieces and often with Urip too in the evening.

When he had opened the gate in the garden wall, Mangun let go of her hand.

"It's better not to be afraid," he said.

And there was the time of the cane fires, not just one by accident but again and again, one after the other, arson!

"Damnation, damnation!" Papa said. "All that good sugar!"

Rick heard the adults talk about it, about how "the population" was dissatisfied, how there might even be a rebellion. And every day behind the mill Papa and the other gentlemen practiced pistol shooting with a cardboard target.

Then Papa had called her into his study one evening, Mama had been with him. She looked very pale in those days, she hadn't said anything, just stared ahead of her without even looking at Rick.

"Listen, Rick, if something should happen and you'd have to leave, you must go with Mangun and do exactly as he tells you. No questions and none of your usual talking back, just obedience. He will take care of you."

"But . . ." Rick said, "and you?"

"I have to stay with the mill," he said shortly.

"And . . . and . . . Mama?"

He hesitated a moment. "Mama would stay with me."

At first Rick had been silent—she could never talk well with her father—but then she burst out, "And me? What about me? Why do I have to go alone? Why do I have to go? Where? Why?"

"There you go already," he said impatiently, "starting to argue about it right off. It isn't even sure that you'll have to go, only if it's necessary for your own . . ." He suddenly stopped. "If it's best that way—can't you understand?"

"Yes," Rick said, "you mean when they come to murder us." Then he had become even angrier.

Her parents never drove out at night in those days, but they often talked until late with people from the mill. The house was closed up at nightfall in the normal way, but Mangun did not go home as usual, he stayed with Karto the watchman under the window of Rick's room. Urip was there too, and Rick sat with the three old servants on their mats on the back veranda. There wasn't a lamp burning anywhere.

"Light shows the way for good and for bad people," Karto always said.

But it wasn't dark outside, for there was another cane fire going somewhere. A threatening red glow lit up the sky, and it was burning hot as if from the fire, although there was a high wind blowing from the mountain. The wind carried little charred pieces of cane leaf, and ashes.

There was a suffocating smell of smoke. The fire couldn't be far away.

Tong-tongs sounded everywhere, the drums made of hollow tree trunks which hung in even the smallest villages. They were very loud: a dark, exciting sound in the night. It went with the fire, with flames and wildly flickering shadows, with heavy yellow smoke, angry men shouting from wide-open mouths.

The wind carried the sound, from nearby, from far away. At times it seemed as if a tong-tong were hanging in the garden and men standing right there beating and beating and beating on it.

The servants were stirring their coffee.

"Do you want coffee too, heart of mine?" Urip asked.

But Rick didn't like their black coffee. "No," she said. Just "no," she never did that, it wasn't proper, but she felt so restless, not afraid really, but angry and very restless. Why were they beating the tong-tongs so hard? Why did

they start fires? Why did they want to kill her parents?
What had her parents done? Let them come! "Come on,
just come—" She clamped her teeth together hard.

Urip put down her cup with a clatter and suddenly
said the worst word she knew: "the devil," "the devil," several times.

"Please be still." It was as if Mangun wanted to listen
without her interrupting. After a while it became quieter,
the fire seemed to be dying down. They weren't beating
the tong-tongs quite so hard any more; then they stopped
altogether.

Slowly the night sky became dark and still and cool
again. The wind went on blowing steadily; water was mur-
muring in the ditches of the garden. Urip brought out
Rick's striped blanket, put it around her and took Rick's
head in her lap.

"Go to sleep," Mangun said to her in his soft voice.
"Don't be afraid."

Urip's legs were hard and bony under her sarong, but
Rick lay there feeling safe and nice. She listened to their
talk, she couldn't understand everything when they spoke
Malayan so quickly and softly, but she heard Karto the
watchman say: "When you reach that place, you mustn't
take the road to the east but to the west."

To the west lay the mountain.

"You must go west, friend!" "Friend"—they always said
that to each other.

And Mangun's cool voice repeated: "From there I go
west. I understand, friend."

Rick stirred. "Don't be afraid," he had said. If it had to

be, she was ready to go with him on the road to the mountain, without . . . She sighed, and fell asleep on Urip's hard knees.

But it hadn't been necessary to leave, no one came to murder them, and the cane fires stopped.

And of death Rick was also afraid.

Not of the way the old gentleman had died, old and sick; there was nothing frightening about that.

But one day Rose the seamstress was suddenly dead, in the morning. Her husband, the clerk from the factory, came to tell Papa and Mama.

"Yes, just like that . . . she was choking, and suddenly . . ." he said, squatting in front of them, and he nodded several times.

When Papa and Mama asked further, he said the same thing again.

He was a stiff little man, strong and thin, neatly dressed; he stared straight ahead without any expression on his face.

Mama got very excited. "But why didn't you call us? Or Urip, or Mangun? The laundryman? He lives right next to you!"

But he just repeated, "Yes . . . suddenly . . ."

They needed a doctor, but the Dutch doctor in town had been ill for some time, and the Javanese doctor had left that same day on a journey. Papa and Mama went to look, but Rose was dead, and she had to be buried before sunset.

In the afternoon Rick and the nieces sat on the steps of

the back veranda stringing white melattis together for the funeral. Urip had shown them how, then she had gone with Mama to the linen closet and a moment later she went by carrying a roll of unbleached muslin.

"For Rose, to dress her," Assi whispered importantly.

Rick looked at her. Rose in unbleached muslin! So ugly, grayish with black dots, and such a stale smell!

"And why not in her own batik kain and jacket? And her slip with the gold sovereigns?"

"Not allowed," Assi said.

"And her rings and earrings and flowers?"

"Not allowed either," Assi said.

Suddenly Rick couldn't stand Assi, and she went on fixing the flowers without saying another word. They were to be beautiful long white garlands, for Rose.

After a while she saw the priest come, and other men; Mangun had already gone to Rose's house. Urip came to get the garlands. Rick and the nieces wanted to go along, but Urip said abruptly, "You must stay here," and took the melattis from them. "Stay here," she said once again.

And so they remained, sitting very close to each other, Rick in the middle.

There was no one in the garden, the sun was already low, the trees darkened and also the mountain beyond the garden wall. A little bat was fluttering around and around.

After a while a procession entered the garden. A bier on which Rose lay, covered with brown batik kains and cloths, and over them the delicate white garlands which the children had made. Four men carried the bier, the others followed shuffling along. One man held a paper parasol over the end of the bier where Rose's head lay.

There were no women.

The priest sang his prayers and beat a little drum hanging from his neck on a ribbon.

Assi began to cry softly, and Nèng said, "I'm scared, I'm very scared." Rick sat between them, her heart beating very fast.

The bier was so dark, all those dark men behind it, moving through the garden in the late light. That was Rose—Rose of the flowers and the rings and batik work and pink jackets—wrapped in grayish muslin and dead.

When they had passed, Assi started to cry even harder until Urip came and took both nieces away with her. And a few days later Rose's husband vanished.

"Where is . . . ?"

"What happened . . . ?"

"Oh . . . terrible . . . terrible!"

The servants stood together and whispered, and then they quickly went back to their work. Papa and Mama also whispered together. Papa called all the servants into his study. Rick tried to hear what they were saying; they all said the same: "I don't know," "I don't understand," "perhaps." "Perhaps" was the end of it.

Had Rose been murdered? Had she been murdered by her husband?

Everyone thought so, but no one said it aloud. One careless word and the police would come. Policemen in the big house! The humiliation! For the master and the lady and the miss, and especially for Mangun because he was Number One, and for all the others without exception, down to the smallest kitchen boy. And so no one spoke, no one knew, no one wanted to know.

Yet there it was, unmentionable. At times it made Rick afraid to go to bed; and during the day too, in a quiet room or in the abandoned garden, her heart started beating with quick, short beats right up in her throat.

Rose had been murdered.

One evening at dusk she had gone to find Mangun. He stood on the landing in front of the lamp room, staring into the garden. He looked so old and frail, as if he wouldn't be able to stand up straight in a storm.

"Mangun, what's going to happen now?" Rick asked.

But this time he didn't tell her not to be afraid, he just said, "Don't speak about it, it is all over now."

And that's what it was: over. Rose was dead, buried in the ground. The husband of Rose was gone; if no one looked for him, no one would find him. Only the white cockatoo was still there. Mangun had taken it because none of the others had wanted it.

"Perhaps it has plucked her soul from her lips," they said.

A GOOD AND SAFE WORD: OVER. But it never lasted long. When one thing was over, another came along. And the worst was still ahead.

It started one evening at cards. During the preceding days there had been a stream of letters received and read aloud, there had been raised eyebrows, whispering and angry altercations.

Then Aunt Nancy arrived with her maid and all her trunks and her pretty striped hatbox.

She had come to say goodbye, for she was going to Holland. She had said "yes" after all, or almost yes. She was going to divorce Uncle Rudolf and marry Uncle Fred, but first she had to go to Holland for a year and only then could she marry Uncle Fred—that was the proper way; and it was all a secret, a deep, dark secret.

"It is perhaps better that you know, Rick," Mama said, "but you must promise that you won't talk about it with anybody, especially not with the servants, do you hear?— nobody!"

Rick was prepared to promise solemnly, to swear; "as sure as I'll die," the servants always said. It wasn't at all necessary not to tell them, for they knew already.

"How did it happen?" she asked, since Mama was so communicative. "Is Uncle Rudolf a bad man?"

"Uncle Rudolf bad! Now what sort of an idea is that? No, of course not!" Mama said indignantly. "You mean because of Aunt Nancy's . . . ?" "Divorce" was not a word to say aloud. "It's sad enough . . . Aunt Nancy thinks that she loves Uncle Fred more than Uncle Rudolf, and with no children perhaps it is indeed best." But then she suddenly checked herself, startled at her own words.

Uncle Fred came too, unexpectedly, for a few days, with only Buyung along. Mama was upset. "You can't do that, Fred—under the same roof!"

He had to sleep in the guest pavilion and Aunt Nancy slept in a guest room of the house. When no one was looking, they kissed.

Uncle Fred looked so young, radiant actually, all the time. Aunt Nancy too, but not always. Buyung looked depressed.

"Serves him right," Urip said. "The new lady will surely throw him out!"

That evening there was a party—everything had to go on normally, Mama said. The tables and the decks of cards and the boxes of mother-of-pearl chips were put out on the front veranda, around the couch with the Flora statue, because they might have some dancing later. White butterfly orchids and maidenfern hung from the cornucopia.

All the lamps were lit.

Mama wore her lilac silk dress with the bow, and the black medallion on a choker around her neck. Aunt Nancy wore her prettiest dress, pink tulle, a long flounced skirt and a ruffled top which left her arms and neck bare. She had a pink gauze fan with a row of pale-blue cockades along the edge; when she closed it, it looked like one big cockade on a handle. And there was a light-blue cockade pinned in her high blond coiffure. "My Lady the Marshal," Uncle Fred said, looking at her, but there were already too many people present. He sat at one table, Aunt Nancy with Papa and two other gentlemen at another, "not at the same table!"—Mama didn't want that— "and please don't look at each other all the time!"

Aunt Nancy obediently turned her back to Uncle Fred and to Flora with the butterfly orchids and the greens. If Uncle Fred looked over at her, she couldn't see him. One of the gentlemen at her table was an officer like Uncle Fred, but he was a doctor and very fat. They played omber and used odd words—spadille, manille, basta and ponto and gasco. Every now and then one of them said "a little one," and all four of them laughed and put a chip in the box.

Supper was brought to the tables: Mangun and the second houseboy and the lamp boy came around with the large trays and Rick was allowed to help them serve. Now when someone shook hands with her, she curtsied as Aunt Nancy had shown her.

During the sherbet, a light-pink sherbet in tulip glasses with whipped cream and candied fruit on top, the fat doctor began talking about Ngawi, about the soldiers. At Ngawi there was a disciplinary army camp, and the rattan was still used there quite frequently. Before a whipping, a soldier had to put on tight shorts and was bound to a post, with his hands tied high. There had to be a doctor present in case the man collapsed; the doctor could order them to stop if he thought that the man could stand no more.

His predecessor had been one of those softhearted fellows, but he didn't believe in being soft—it didn't serve any purpose.

"When you give a chap a thrashing, do a good job of it, I always say—just about within an inch of his life is the place to stop."

Rick looked at him. He was sitting there so heavily and quietly in his white uniform, with his cards in his hands. He looked as if he were chatting about the weather, but not to Papa and the other gentleman; he was addressing Aunt Nancy only. Aunt Nancy sat very still; she stared at the green cloth of the card table and put down her cards. She looked so odd, as if her hair had come undone and her dress been wrinkled. Once she took up her cards, then she quickly put them on the table again.

"Then when he is taken down I have to inspect the wounds. I must say, a rattan makes nice wounds, depends very much on the man who does the thrashing. The warden always says, "if we'd give him a rubdown now with some red peppers, sir, he'd be tamed for keeps—"

"Dear doctor," Papa said in his coldest voice, "spare us, if you please." And the other gentleman looked annoyed too. But Aunt Nancy pushed her chair back, stood for a moment between it and the table, then took hold of her fan which was dangling from a ribbon around her wrist.

She didn't look at anyone. What was she going to do? Rick came closer— Oh yes, fine, she thought. Give him a smack, hard, as hard as you can—come on, please, hard! and she clenched her fists.

"I don't wish to play with you any longer," Aunt Nancy only said, not even very loud, but clear, clear enough for everyone to hear. "The other gentlemen must excuse me, please."

She turned around and walked slowly and stiffly along the veranda with the fan in her hand. When she passed Rick, she started and put out her hand.

"Come along, Riquette."

Before they had left the veranda, Rick could hear two angry men's voices and one of them was Uncle Fred's. She wanted to go back, but Aunt Nancy didn't let go of her hand. She pulled Rick along and started to run, tripping several times over her long skirt. She stopped only when she reached the staircase of the back veranda, and her breath came rapidly.

"Why were you standing there, Riquette? Did you hear what he said? So evil . . . so evil . . ." She had let go of her fan, which dangled from the ribbon again, she let go of Rick's hand too and clasped her hands together.

"What can we do? What can we do? We have to do

something, but we can't, the world is so full of evil," she said with real despair, and sighed deeply.

At their feet, disavowing her words, lay the garden in the moonlight: the hedges of clipped bushes, the two aviaries, the carriage room to the left with the row of manggas and the other tall, motionless trees; beyond the garden wall the silhouette of the mountain, pure and tight against the sky.

There was an overwhelming scent of flowers; somewhere a kemuning tree was in bloom—little white flowers which open in the moonlight.

And everything seemed to be so still, so silver and white. Not the ordinary world of here and always, but of somewhere else. As if in that pure light ugliness had become beauty, imperfection perfection, and all evil forgiven.

But somewhere there was a post with a man tied to it, and a warden and a doctor looking on.

One and the other. But it couldn't be; not good and evil together. Either one or the other. Not together.

Rick tried to take Aunt Nancy's hand, but she didn't pay attention to her and held her hands away.

"Yes," she said as if continuing from where she had stopped before, "yes, we can do something. We can be good ourselves, we must change and be good—just that. You'll see."

Rick looked at her. "But you *are* good," she said, "and Uncle Fred is too!" And Papa and Mama, she thought, and the old gentleman, and Uncle Rudolf also, Mama said, and Mangun, and Buyung—she suddenly knew a whole list of good people.

Aunt Nancy bent over as if she were going to take her in her arms, but she pushed her away instead, although gently.

"You'd better go to sleep now, Riquette," she said, and picked up her fan and her flounced skirt and slowly walked down the stairs into the garden.

Where was she going? Was she going for a walk in the moonlight?

She walked quietly, as if it were perfectly normal, to the guest pavilion where Uncle Fred was staying, entered the dark gallery and did not reappear.

Rick stayed where she was, looking after her. Now she is sitting up straight in one of the rocking chairs, Rick thought, in the dark, in her pink tulle dress with the blue cockade in her hair and the other blue cockade in her hand, and she is waiting for him. And when he comes she stands up and goes toward him in the dark, puts her arms around him and whispers, "Fred, we must change and be good—just that. You'll see."

And what would Uncle Fred say then?

The following morning at breakfast the fight with Papa took place.

Uncle Fred had left. He had driven off very early in the morning with Buyung in one of Papa's dog carts, without a spare horse—that was never allowed!—without a word, without saying goodbye to anyone.

The four of them were sitting around the dining-room table, Papa, Mama, Aunt Nancy and Rick; nobody said very much. They had almost finished breakfast when Papa started talking, a bit mockingly as he would sometimes, but at the same time so excited and annoyed that he forgot to send Rick away.

"My dear Nancy, are we allowed to know what's going on? Where has Fred gone? Such a scene with that old doctor—was that necessary? And Fred, that idiot, going you one better and challenging him seriously! Did you know? Did Fred tell you? Where did you suddenly vanish to last night? Imagine, a duel over our beautiful Nancy, for that's what it comes down to, isn't it?"

Aunt Nancy sat straight, but with her head bowed, and slowly some tears streaked down her cheeks and fell on her breakfast plate. Papa stopped, startled.

"No, I didn't know," she said, "but don't worry, Fred won't fight any duels now because of your beautiful Nancy!"

Papa and Mama looked at each other.

Aunt Nancy sat there so strangely with tears now running down and down her face, and then she said in a tight, cold voice, "Fred and I have broken. Fred has left and I am going back to Rudolf."

No one spoke.

Then something happened; it was as if it weren't Papa but somebody else in his chair, somebody shorter and heavier, with bigger hands, a reddish face, who said slowly as if he were surprised, "And you let him go off alone, just like that? Well, damn it all, Nancy, damn it all!" and he hit the table hard with his fist, got up without another word and walked off the veranda.

"But Ab, but Ab, what has come over you!" Mama cried.

She jumped up from her chair, put her arms around Aunt Nancy, and they wept together. Then they went to Aunt Nancy's room to pack, without Rick.

A stable boy came through the garden with two horses.

And late in the morning the carriage drove up for Aunt Nancy.

Mangun had raised one of the striped screens on the front veranda, that way Mama and Rick could see her off properly. Papa hadn't returned.

Aunt Nancy was wearing her white silk travel coat and she held a large bouquet of roses which Mama had put in her hands to comfort her a little. She immediately got into the carriage and sat on the back bench beside her striped hatbox, opposite her own maid in a brown sarong and bright jacket.

The old coachman, in a kind of uniform of black and white, with a flat lacquered hat on top of his kerchief, was waiting on the box; a groom, dressed like the coachman, stood in front of the horses and held their bridles.

Rick and Mama were at the bottom of the marble staircase, they had said goodbye, everything was done, Aunt Nancy could drive off.

For one moment nothing happened. The dark carriage with the black team and the four people stood still in the harsh light, against the background of the green garden, and it was all drawn as clearly as a cut-out silhouette.

One moment, and in it everything was still possible: Aunt Nancy could put the roses down, step out again and come back. She could hold the roses in her hands and drive off, not come back, never come back. She could still choose.

One short moment, but a moment which could never pass—everything waited, it was for ever and ever.

Forever Aunt Nancy was sitting in the carriage not knowing whether to get out and stay or go.

Forever Rick and Mama were standing at the steps in the burning sun.

Then the old coachman carefully turned his head sideways—he didn't look around, that wouldn't have been proper—and immediately Aunt Nancy said, "Yes . . . yes . . . yes, all right . . ." The coachman touched the horses with his whip, they shook their heads; the groom had already let go of them, he jumped aside and climbed onto the box next to the coachman.

The horses pulled, the wheels crunched on the pebbles.

Aunt Nancy didn't wave or call out as she usually did. She held the roses stiffly and said, "Anna, Rick, adieu."

Why did she say that, "adieu," it sounded so sad, so— "I commend thee to God," and everything over forever. "Over" wasn't always a good word.

Anyway, now she was gone and now they were no longer friends with Aunt Nancy.

UNCLE FRED LEFT FOREVER TOO. He did fight his duel with the fat doctor after all—"he's a Don Quixote," Papa said. Nobody got hurt, but dueling was no longer allowed and they were both punished severely: room arrest, a very humiliating thing. Then Uncle Fred— "he's a hothead," Papa said—resigned his commission and he was going away, not to Holland but really away, to Australia, and forever. Someone was helping him, he would get a job there inspecting horses.

He came to the house, without his own horse which he had already sold since he was no longer an officer; without the beautiful saddles, without a groom— "without a penny

79

to his name," Papa said. He brought only Buyung, who would have to stay with them in the big house because Uncle Fred could not take him along. Colored people were not allowed to live in Australia, neither yellow people nor brown, black or red—only white, white is no color.

The first evening Urip was already in a terrible state because Buyung had come to stay. Everything was just horrid.

Uncle Fred seemed another man; he laughed differently and looked different, he was so quiet, and then again he had endless discussions with Papa and Mama, loud and angry ones, and they looked furiously at each other like the jalak birds in the garden, and never stopped. Papa was the worst.

Rick couldn't quite hear what it was all about; but one evening she was awakened by her parents' voices coming from Mama's dressing room, which was next to her bedroom. As always Papa was angry, Mama soothing—or was she scolding him? Rick didn't quite know what to do, to eavesdrop on a conversation wasn't proper. She listened when she was in the same room, but then they could see her and it was up to them to be careful. This was different. Should she put her fingers in her ears? But then she heard her own name and couldn't help listening.

Mama said: "Have you forgotten how much she loved our Rick?"

"Nonsense," Papa said. "You know as well as I do, it wasn't our Rick but a child born from her own imagination, perhaps a child of Fred's and hers. Women like Nancy . . ."

Mama interrupted him. "You are unjust to Nancy, she only wanted to do her duty, it isn't her fault that Fred has acted so foolishly. You used to like Nancy so."

"Yes, certainly," Papa said, "I used to like Nancy."

"Yes," Mama said, "I'm aware of that, Ab."

Papa laughed his scornful little laugh. "Shall we avoid getting sidetracked?" he asked. "Nancy is a charming woman, and it is very good of her to go back to her husband, only she is a bit late with it. Are you—" he was getting more and more excited again—"are you all completely blind, Nancy and you too? Can't you see what's going to happen to Fred? That he's just a schoolboy, in spite of all his talk, a vulnerable boy—we can be thankful that he hasn't already . . ."

"No, no, don't say it!" Mama cried. "Don't say it aloud!"

Then, because Mama's voice sounded so sad, Papa said, "All right, I won't say anything more, perhaps he will come back in one piece from Australia someday. I can make him supervisor of the scales at the mill."

Rick was horrified. Imagine! Uncle Fred as supervisor of weighing—that was no job for him!

After a while Papa added, "If Buyung could only go with him, then at least he'd have a nursemaid to keep an eye on him. Come, we'd better go to bed, Ann."

Rick heard the short sucking sound of the screen doors turning; he was holding the little black-and-gold Singapore doors open for Mama. "But why don't you stop him, Ab? You have to stop him. Keep him from going away!" Mama said.

And Papa said shortly, but there was nothing cold or

mocking left in his voice, "We can't keep each other from going away, Ann."

Before she fell asleep, Rick thought, adults are that way, they're not angry with each other, just sad about each other, but it looks the same. And . . . is it all really Aunt Nancy's fault?

And "Riquette"—no, she wasn't Riquette.

And . . . why do I love Papa more than anyone else now?

Next day Rick walked through the house with Uncle Fred, along the closed back gallery; Uncle Fred went a little ahead of her with his head lowered, staring as if he were lost in thought. The big lemon trees in the garden were in blossom, and on the dining-room table stood an old blue bowl full of branches in bloom. They were picked from the tree, which bore only bitter fruit anyway. The sharp, spicy, sweet scent had saturated the whole room; a few black bees had flown in and were buzzing around the white flowers. The little buzzing sound made the gallery seem even bigger and higher and quieter than usual, the marble of the floor more deeply gleaming—and everything seemed to be waiting in suspense.

Uncle Fred suddenly stopped and turned halfway around toward Rick. He didn't speak immediately. His tired eyes lay so deep in their sockets and he had pressed his lips together, the way he used to, which made his cheeks all hollow. After a while he said, "When I'm gone, could you have a look at Buyung sometimes, talk a bit with him, and see to it that that angel Urip—" he always said that— "doesn't do him any harm? I'm worried about Buyung."

"I will look after Buyung when you're gone," Rick said quietly, "but . . . but . . . why are you going, can't you live without . . . do you love . . ." Aunt Nancy so much, she wanted to say, but suddenly she didn't dare say her name aloud—"do you love Buyung so much?" But that wasn't what she had wanted to ask him at all!

At first he didn't answer; he looked at her in astonishment, then he became angry—why had she opened her mouth!

"Yes, I love Buyung, of course I love Buyung, he is faithful. Do you know what that means? Or are you too young to know?" he asked with a deep frown.

But now Rick became angry too; he didn't have to talk to her in that tone! "Yes, of course I know," she answered shortly, and then she remembered a sentence she had read somewhere or someone had read to her, she didn't know where or by whom: Be faithful until death, it started. And without realizing she said it aloud, trying to think in the meantime what came next; but she had forgotten.

"Be faithful until death."

"Yes," Uncle Fred said, "that is what I mean."

And suddenly he didn't seem to be angry with her any more. He stood still and he looked at her so oddly, so intensely, as if he saw her for the first time in his life, then he shook his head about something, stared into space and didn't say anything more. After a while he walked away and left her there.

Rick was standing near the bowl with the flowers, thinking; the white flowers were motionless, perfumed, the little black bees were buzzing and circling around. A feeling of powerlessness swept over her like a wave, and a feeling of bitter shame. Now she understood why Papa had raged so much against Aunt Nancy, but it wasn't only Aunt Nancy —no.

They, all of them—they were not a small family. A large family! Suddenly Rick had a whole row of brothers and sisters; there were uncles and aunts and cousins and nephews and nieces on Papa's side, Uncle Fred's side, Mama's side; all the grandparents were still alive—a proud family, respected by everyone. And they were letting one of themselves depart from their midst.

Not to the Holy Land, in armor and on a valiant steed, surrounded by faithful squires, like in the book with the tales of knighthood and chivalry—no.

And the women in the family had not been working for months to make him a sash of silks and gold thread and pearls to be worn over one shoulder, and standards for the lances, and a large velvet purse for his gold—oh no!

They were letting him go—all alone—in an old suit, without a penny to his name, to a dry and sterile land where only kangaroos lived and ostriches without ostrich feathers. No one was stopping him, they didn't even look after him, he, the best of all of them.

A respected family! That was a joke. A contemptible bunch of people they were, nothing else!

And then came the last evening, and the farewell party for Uncle Fred—that was the way he had wanted it. There were so many people, from the sugar mills, from town: all his friends had come, on the train.

He introduced them to Rick, he solemnly gave their

names and hers—my niece Frederica—what was so funny about that?

Aunt Nancy wasn't there.

First they had a play, a pantomime, not with puppets but with dancers, a very famous troupe from Solo—that way it was a party for the servants too. They all sat on chairs on the lawn, facing the drive with the kanari trees, and the double row of high, light-colored trees was like a backdrop for the stage. All around the lawn wax candles were burning.

The gamelan stood at one side; there was a narrator too. On the other side the servants were seated, Buyung in front, heavy and messy as always, with his wild kerchief. When the three clowns appeared, he laughed very hard. The performance began.

There was Sita the Princess and the heroes, the two brothers Rama and Laksmana; there were evil giants, and good monkeys, and the King of the monkeys, Sugriva, and Hanumat, his aide. And when things became too sad, the three clowns appeared, one a dwarf and a hunchback, one very tall and thin, one short and fat—just as they should be.

First the gamelan played soft and low, and the narrator started the story in his high boyish voice. It sounded like verse in a severe meter. The gamelan joined in all the time, dark and moving, or again in light, airy runs like tinkling bells—but the voice continued over it, tight and measured, telling the story.

Rick sat there with beating heart, thinking of what she had done: she had made a little cushion of melatti flowers on a piece of cardboard; it looked like a white pin cushion and it smelled nice. She had pinned a note to it.

"Dear Uncle Fred, stay here! Your Rick," the note said.

She had put it in his room in the guest pavilion after he had gone out. He would find it after the party. Would he be very annoyed? Would it help, would he want to stay?

That morning Buyung had gone to see him. He had dressed for the occasion, in long black trousers, a black jacket with long sleeves, and a stiff sarong, dark blue with gold thread in it, fastened around his waist with a big knot. He looked as if he'd had a haircut, his dark-blue kerchief had gold thread too, the points stood up straight behind one ear. He had squatted in the front gallery of the guest pavilion and spoken in jerky sentences, as if he couldn't find the proper words.

"I have come . . . I have thought a lot . . . I wanted to tell you . . . I wanted to ask you, sir . . . don't leave us!" Don't leave us people, they said in Malayan.

Uncle Fred had stood next to him.

"You'd better be quiet, Buyung!" First angrily and impatiently, and then again, but much more gently, "Better be quiet, Buyung."

And Buyung had got up. "Then it can't be helped, sir," he had said and left, and had taken off his ceremonial clothes and put them back into his box.

It hadn't helped. Uncle Fred hadn't listened to Buyung.

The dancers danced, the gamelan played, the narrator spoke.

If Aunt Nancy, the Aunt Nancy of the past, were only

here in her big white shawl with the long fringe, she could have taken a chair next to Uncle Fred's and said softly through the gamelan music, "Why to Australia, Daddy longlegs? Don't you remember early summer and the linden tree in front of the church all in bloom?" She had said that once, about the linden. Would it have helped? Would he have listened to the linden?

Or his friends, if they . . . Rick looked around at where they were sitting amidst the others. That one perhaps? Or he? Or he?

A moment came in which the dancer, Sita the Princess, was standing on the stage alone. She did not move, she stood with her arms and legs against her body, straight in her stiff costume: in the long brown batik kain, so long that a point of the front ran between her legs making a train in back; the tight velvet bodice which left shoulders and arms bare, the wide belt around her waist. She had a gilded winged helmet on her head, all her jewelry was gold: a buckle, bracelets with bird and snake heads around the upper and lower arms, a necklace with three half-moons, earrings. Garlands of flowers. Two long, brightly colored sashes hanging from her belt.

Then she started to dance, but she scarcely moved. It was as if her feet hardly left the ground, just bent a little in the ankles, the stiff straight kain hiding whatever movement there was in the knees and hips. Her waist, her breasts and her neck, her set yellow face didn't move either. All movement was concentrated in the arms, the shoulders, elbows and wrists, in the beautiful supple hands which took up the long, hanging silk sashes, twisted them

around, threw them up in the air and caught them again.
She was Sita the Princess, walking . . .

The old gentleman had told Rick about her once. How, long ago, she walked through the woods with the two brothers when they were going into exile. Rama the Prince, her husband, went in front, then she, then the Prince Laksmana; and at times Rama looked around at the two following him. This is before the silver deer lures her away and she falls into the hands of the giant demons, before the battle of the two heroes and the monkeys on one side against the giants on the other, before they all lie down badly wounded, before she mounts the burning pyre. And so that Rama would see his brother Laksmana well when he looked around again, and to let Laksmana see his brother Rama well, perhaps for the last time—for she knew of all the sorrow awaiting them—Sita no longer walked between those two she loved. She went to walk alone at the edge of the road where there were stones, mud and thorns.

So the dancer walked at the edge of the lawn with her stiff little steps. Her hands and the two sashes said what she felt, all she felt in her heart—love and sorrow, dark forebodings, and, above all, tenderness.

While Rick was looking at her she suddenly knew that nothing could be done, that Uncle Fred would go away and that they shouldn't try to hold him back. He hadn't listened to Buyung, he wouldn't listen to the linden tree either, nor to Papa and Mama, nor to his friends; not to him, and not to him, and also not to the note.

The dancer had gone. The battle began between heroes,

monkeys and angry giants. The men circled each other with springy jumping steps, shot their arrows from huge bows, and fell down dying in the green grass. When the clowns came back Buyung no longer laughed; he kept staring at Uncle Fred with his dark brooding eyes.

After a while they all got up and went into the house. The big house with its white pillars was lying there so peacefully between the trees, and it was waiting for them. On the front veranda all the lamps were lit, the light fell into the garden, and the round couch with Flora and her cornucopia full of flowers was standing on the black star, for there would be dancing later. As soon as she could, Rick went around the house in the dark and down to the guest pavilion, to take away the flower cushion and the note.

And so Uncle Fred did leave for Australia. Was it a lucky day? What was the direction of the Snake? Why wasn't the old gentleman there any more?

Buyung stayed, the old coachman had fallen ill and now he was their coachman.

THE HEAVY TARRED DOORS of the carriage house were always locked from the outside with a chain and a padlock. There were no other doors, just a row of little windows high up on one wall. The mangga trees stood outside them, and the pale green and yellow reflections from their leaves fell in through the dusty windowpanes.

In those days Rick liked to hide sometimes. All she had to do was go into the carriage house and pull the big doors shut behind her. The chain often hung loose; nobody paid any attention to that.

Next to the door stood Papa's two dog carts, a black one

and a brown one. Then came the four-wheeled coach with its permanent black top and rolled-up black leather curtains and hard, unpleasant benches. On the other side stood the victoria, which was for afternoon drives; it had a folding top, a wide back bench with springs and a stiff little bench behind the high coachman's box. Then there was the yellow lacquered hunting dray, and a light carriage with wheels far apart, which was used when the roads were very muddy.

And at the back of the carriage house stood the old travel coach. It wasn't used any more, and no one knew to whom it had belonged or how it had got there. It had always been standing there, Mangun said, from very long ago.

The coach looked like the victoria, only much bigger, with a folding leather top hanging in straps mounted on big springs. It was lacquered dark blue with yellow borders, and inside it was upholstered in beige, a rough beige material with holes in it made by the mice. Running boards on each side could be folded back, the high box had a brass railing running around it, and there was a leather pillow on the coachman's seat. At the back was a wide running board for the footmen, supported by graceful cast-iron curlecues. And the lanterns! Such beautiful lanterns, big and square, with brass tops and brass columns at the corners.

Rick got in and sat down on the wide back bench. She rested her hands on it and felt the indentations, the four folds coming together with a smooth leather button. She rocked up and down, and the coach swung in its straps and squeaked. She leaned back.

Buyung sat on the box and they drove with four horses,

not the ordinary ones, but four huge horses, pitch-black, with their necks arched and their manes and tails waving. Buyung held all the reins in his big left hand. On the box in a brass holder stood the beautiful whip, a long thin one with a red tassel. He took it in his right hand at times; he didn't whip the horses but just touched them with the tassel to guide them: to the left or to the right, around a corner, slower or faster.

They drove.

The big Post Road—the road to the town—past the relay post with the white pillars and the sloping roof; there were no relay horses, they didn't need them. Across the big bridge—no, with the ferry across the wide, brown, churning river, to the town, and on.

The big Post Road, wide and dusty, and without end. On the high shoulders tamarind trees grew, with their transparent green foliage; the wind blew through it and all those fine little leaves vibrated.

Now they drove through the teak woods with their sapless trees, nothing but trunks, and on the road lay the big leathery leaves which had fallen; when the wheels drove through them, they made a sound of paper tearing, but much louder.

The town Ngawi. They drove past a large building behind a fence with sharp iron points; it looked like a prison—no, it was the camp for the soldiers.

Rick sat up straight with a start and listened. She didn't hear anything. They had already passed it, but there, on the road, the doctor was walking. Rick had almost forgotten him, but now she recognized him immediately. He was coming straight toward them.

She leaned over and whispered, "Buyung!"

Buyung understood immediately. He reined in the horses, he pulled until they had almost halted but not quite, they drove on very slowly, almost at a walk, the coach creaking and swaying, until they were quite close.

The doctor was wearing a clean white suit. How big and fat he was, from so close up. "Yes, Buyung." Her lips hardly moved.

Buyung took the whip out of the holder, not the thin one with the red tassel but a short, heavy whip, he lifted it— "now"—and hit the doctor across the face. One lash from left to right, and with a quick twist of his wrist another one, from right to left. Crisscross.

The doctor stood still, his face was bleeding badly, the red blood dripped onto his white suit, but he didn't say anything.

Buyung put the whip away, he was panting. Rick leaned back with a deep sigh.

The horses pulled, they drove on again, through teak forests and then through an open plain, rice fields, cane fields, little villages, a town. At a fork Buyung turned down a side road—that was where Aunt Nancy lived. They stopped; Rick hesitated a moment, then she got out, walked around the house and through the garden and the orchard. It seemed a long walk.

In the green porcelain tea pavilion over the lotus pond, the Aunt Nancy of before was sitting.

Nothing had changed. She was wearing a bébé of blue batiste, thin and cool, with shiny spots from the ironing. Rick sat down close to her on the low red-lacquered stool, with her cheek against the batiste sleeve.

She sighed, she was sitting so nicely, she had been sitting that way for a long time, for years and years, she had never been away.

She wanted to tell Aunt Nancy about the doctor, that everything was all right now. But when she said, "the fat doctor," Aunt Nancy asked, surprised, "what fat doctor?"

Rick was confused and it took her a moment to understand. Of course, this was before; there was no fat doctor.

Aunt Nancy sat quietly looking at her with her light-blue eyes and dark pupils.

"Why aren't you my child?"

Rick slapped Aunt Nancy's knees with both hands. "But I am your child!" And they both began to laugh, as they used to. Aunt Nancy pulled her into her arms and rocked her.

"Riquette!" she said. "Of course you're my child, sweet Riquette!"

It was a pity that she said "Riquette," because now Rick remembered that she didn't mean her with that, but the other child. Suddenly she remembered everything. She knew too that now was not before. Now cannot be before, and it cannot be after, it can only be now. And now was not a nice time.

She pulled back and sat up straight on the red stool, away from Aunt Nancy. "Is the old Dragon of Happiness still alive?" she asked politely.

"I expect so," Aunt Nancy said. She poured tea in the beautiful thin cups without saucers, and pushed toward Rick the tin of red-and-white sugar cakes she liked so much.

"No, thank you, Aunt Nancy," Rick said, "thank you, I'm sorry, I have to go on, Buyung is waiting for me with the coach-and-four. You see, I have so far to go still."

She got up, made a neat curtsy, and without looking back she walked away over the little bridge, through the orchard and the garden. She climbed into the coach; Buyung had been waiting patiently. They drove along the big Post Road. They came to mountains, with a large plume of smoke rising from one of them. Here were the two palaces where the sultans lived; one of them had a hundred and ten children. And farther on were the temples. The Prambanan with the story of Sita, the brothers, the monkeys and the giants. The Burubudur, with the life of Buddha, all the different lives of Buddha. The thousand little temples, and another one, and yet another. In one of these, in the dark, were three seated statues, silent, and at the feet of one two deer played.

The road became steeper; they were on their way to the mountain pass and to the house with the heliotrope and the mulberry trees. And in front of the house, under the crooked tree, sat "he with the elephant's head," and farther on Shiva was dancing near the well, and still farther on was the Dièng. But the old gentleman was no longer there.

"No, no, take the other road, you'd better take the northern road, Buyung."

The big Post Road, and they went north, along the sea, quite close to the sea, the waves of the surf beat on the edge of the road. The two horses on the right-hand side were afraid and pressed sideways against the others. Then Buyung took the whip—it was the thin one again with the red tassel—and when the horses felt the tassel they were no longer afraid. And the mountains appeared again, so many mountains, a town, and mountains. And they came to the capital, the white palace of the Governor General—of the Big Master, Mangun said, the real one, the others were only imitation masters.

And in the palace, in a white marble hall, a ball was being held. There was dancing, and so many people, all so beautifully dressed! The ladies held up their trains with little loops, one finger in the loop. Musicians played on violins; one was blowing on a flute. Five hundred candles were burning in crystal chandeliers. But there was Uncle Fred! Tall and slender, all in black, with gold cords and tassels hanging from one shoulder—gala uniform, that was called.

He stood in front of her and bowed.

"Niece Frederica." He was wearing white suede gloves. Rick was tall, and slender too, and her dress was of white, softly gleaming satin, with—yes, with a train. And she had on white satin shoes with silver bows. Around her neck she wore her Sunday necklace of red garnets, but now the stones were big and they sparkled. And she felt the earrings in her ears, very heavy, red.

Uncle Fred leaned over and tapped one earring with his finger, then the other. The suede of his glove touched her ear lobes. He laughed; he was as gay as before.

"My, my!" he said softly, and blinked at her.

She remembered that he used to say that, and it made her laugh. She gave him her hand; she was wearing white lace mitts.

Then they danced. They waltzed, in both directions, she could dance beautifully and even without counting—one-two-three. She held her satin train up with the loop around her finger.

But she couldn't stay, she didn't understand why, but she had been told that she could not stay.

And so she was driving on again, the long road in the swaying coach, the long, quiet, dusty Post Road without end.

They went along the sea, and now the horses on the left were afraid of the waves. They didn't pass the mountain with the plume of smoke again, they took a detour through the plains, through hills and teak forests. Everywhere it was silent; dust hung over the road. It darkened.

The Spessart mountains from the storybook! And Rick was the German countess in disguise. She wore a dress of taffeta now, green with balloon sleeves, and a green cape with a hood; a veil too so that no one would notice she wasn't really the countess. Suddenly, with a jolt, the coach stopped.

The robbers! So many! They dragged Buyung from the box. What were they doing to him? She heard a loud rustling in the dry teak leaves beside the road, but she couldn't see a thing.

Now it was quiet. Had they killed Buyung? Two robbers climbed onto the box, and two on the running boards, one on each side, and the others rode up to the coach; she heard their horses snort.

What had they done to Buyung? Uncle Fred had told her to take care of him; but wait, under the seat the woman's creese lay, the one the old gentleman had given her. When you stick a creese in someone's back, he dies on the spot.

She remained sitting upright, but felt cautiously for it—yes—would she do it? But which one? The one on the left? Or the one on the right?

And the others? There were so many! What would they do to her afterward? She was terrified, her heart was beating so.

And she was sitting in the old travel coach in the carriage house. The leaves of the mangga trees moved in the sunshine in front of the little windows, light green and yellow. She sat still for a moment, her heart was still racing, why?—she had forgotten. She stood up and let herself fall back against the cushions, several times; and the big heavy coach swayed and creaked as if it were going to fall to pieces. Then she jumped out, peeked around the big doors and stepped outside. No one had seen her. For a moment the sharp sunlight blinded her.

Every now and again, when they didn't go for a drive in the afternoon, when the grass cutters had come with their two huge burdens of grass and maize leaves on bamboo yokes and Buyung had weighed them and distributed them over the stables (there were no more rocks lying around to put under the grass) and Buyung was finished working, the circus could start. All the servants came together in the pasture behind the stables to watch; they sat on the grass in a big circle. Mangun with his wife and their little adopted son, Rick with the two nieces Assi and Nèng, the new seamstress, the housemaid and the lamp boy with their five children (all freshly bathed and

combed), the cook, the laundryman with the long finger-
nail—tut, tut!—and his one old wife, the second houseboy,
three gardeners, two water carriers, two stable boys, the
cowherd and his wife. And Karto, the watchman for the
back, and the other watchman for the front came earlier
than on other days. But Urip didn't come.

In the middle of the pasture stood Buyung. He wore only
a pair of short black trousers and a wide belt tight around
his waist, no kerchief; his hair was short and shaggy. He
held a whip, and the little black monkey from the stables
was perched on his shoulder.

First came the horse acts, with one of the horses from
Papa's dog cart. Buyung had taught it tricks: it could raise
itself on its hind legs, it could also kneel, lie on its back,
jump over fences and through a big bamboo hoop, and even
hold up a foot like a dog giving its paw. Buyung walked next
to it all the while and cracked his whip, but he didn't use it
on the horse; all his animals did what he wanted them to do
anyway.

The little monkey watched attentively; as long as all
went well he was content and grinned and winked. But
when the horse made a mistake or was too slow and
Buyung scolded it, the monkey looked worried too,
wrinkled up its face and said "te-te-te." Then it suddenly
embraced Buyung's head in a surge of pure love and became very excited and jumped up and down and almost fell
to the ground. It took part in the last two numbers too.

The horse sat down with its forelegs stretched out; a
bamboo table was put in front of it on the grass, and the
monkey sat opposite it on top of the table. They both had

napkins tied around their necks and then they had dinner together. Buyung put two bananas on the table, a big green one for the horse and a little yellow one for the monkey. Snorting and feeling with its lips, the horse picked up the banana and pushed it against the table into its mouth. It drooled terribly but it couldn't help that. The monkey held its banana neatly in its paws, peeled it and broke off a piece at a time, eating quickly with loud smacks. Then it sat up straight and looked to see how far the horse had got with its banana.

Everyone thought this was a beautiful act! And the last act was the horse walking alone, with the monkey on its back, to the locked stable; it could push away the latches and enter all by itself. Then it neighed, and Buyung came to close the stable door and put the monkey on its long chain; otherwise it would run away into the woods in the night.

Then there was intermission.

They sat in the pasture with Buyung, and there was the confection man with his stand and his bell. They all had a glass of pink lemonade and a cake. The confection man didn't have enough glasses; he rinsed them in a little tin filled with water and then poured again. He was terribly busy, he also had to collect his money and make change, and he made marks on a slate for those who would pay "next month"—and what about Rick? She never had any money, except in her closet in a piggy bank, but she couldn't get that out. Finally Mangun paid for her, everyone watched, and Rick was terribly embarrassed.

And all the time the confection man rang his bell as if he

were still on the road looking for customers. It sounded very gay.

Then came the second part of the program: Buyung and the bull calf. It was a beautiful calf, still young, not very big, light brown and white, with bulging eyes that gleamed and neat little curls on its head in between the beginnings of its horns, like bangs fresh from the hairdresser. And Buyung stood next to it, so dark and solid, with his long dangling arms. He had put the whip aside.

First they just played a bit. The calf tried to butt, and Buyung jumped aside with big grotesque steps like a clown. Then he suddenly stood still with his wide flat feet planted in the grass, his arms hanging down, while he waited for the calf to come closer. He reached out and took hold of its head and pushed it against his body. The calf got angry and pulled and butted. At first Buyung stayed put, holding on; the calf pushed harder and harder and kicked with its hind legs. Then Buyung was pushed forward, faster and faster across the grass; suddenly he sat down, the calf lost its equilibrium and rolled over him. They wrestled awhile and rolled around with each other in the grass.

After that they had to rest. The calf grazed and stared around; it could look extremely stupid. It was standing still, and Buyung went up to it. He bent over—quickly—and put his long dark arms around its four legs, high up, near its body, and slowly, slowly—the muscles of his arms, his neck, his legs, all swelled—slowly he lifted the calf up off the ground. He swayed to and fro as if he would not be able to hold it—only his two feet remained in place; he tried to take a step, staggered, leaned over so far that it looked as if he were going to fall, but then suddenly he walked on, carried, really carried the bull calf halfway to the stables.

They all walked after him, holding their breath; some of the youngest called out yes, no, yes, and counted. When he put the calf down they applauded and cheered and everyone cried "beautiful, wonderful!"

Buyung stood still and looked shy. He was dripping with sweat, and there was blood in the whites of his eyes from the little veins that had burst. He rubbed his face dry with his arm and chased the calf into the stable. "Go to sleep, brother!"

The sun had set. The stable boys went to light the lamps and hang them in the stables, one with the horses, one with the cows, and one with Jacob the bull. The dog-cart horse neighed once more and the monkey made a plaintive sound like a tired child that wants to go to sleep.

Rick walked alone through the garden to the house. It was so peaceful and quiet in the evening. She looked around—what would Uncle Fred have said about the circus?—and suddenly she stood still, she had to stand still, because the ground was no longer solid under her feet and the universe, everything around her, trees and house and mountain and sky, fell soundlessly and without motion into pieces.

She—not Aunt Nancy—*she* was in love with Uncle Fred. How stupid . . . how stupid . . . why had she never realized it before! Then she might perhaps—but there was still time.

"When I'm grown up, I'm going to him with Buyung, to get him, to bring him back, back here with us."

She stood still and straight. It was a solemn moment, like taking a pledge, and the stars were witnesses. Closest stood Orion.

"Orion, are you listening?"

So the days went by, many more days. There had been a letter from Australia, a very short one, also one for Buyung; then one more, and that was the end. One afternoon during tea a man came, a special mailman without a mailbag; he brought only an express letter, something like a telegram.

Papa opened it.

"Rick, go do your piano practice, you can come back later, Mama and I . . ." He gave Mama the letter, she looked and immediately began to cry. "See, do you see now?" she said.

Rick was still there, she looked at them, from one to the other. "But what has happened?" she asked.

Papa swallowed; he wanted to say something, but Mama answered immediately, "Uncle Fred . . . he is not coming back. He has drowned in the sea, swimming, in Australia," and cried. She held her handkerchief against her mouth and then she said again, "See . . . see . . ." Rick and Papa didn't speak, and there they were sitting around the table, the three of them.

Buyung, Rick thought. Who is going to tell Buyung? But Papa had already rung for Mangun.

"Mangun, would you call Buyung?"

Mangun squatted on the ground; he didn't normally do that, only when something extraordinary had happened.

"Buyung already knows, sir," he said, and coughed as if he were going to add something, then he just held up his folded hands in front of his face, slowly and carefully; that too he did only rarely, on solemn occasions. He rose and left.

Rick sat in her chair and rocked. Uncle Fred—Uncle Fred whom she loved, and she couldn't cry about him. Her face, her eyes, her mouth were so dry. Her throat hurt when she swallowed, but there were no tears. Why not?

Papa sat just like Rick; only Mama cried, into a sopping wet handkerchief, and the tears kept rolling down her face.

Rick got up. "You mustn't cry so, Mama!" she said in a hard, reprimanding voice. She went to the garden, but not around the house as always; she went down the marble steps of the front veranda like a stranger who had been there on a visit and was going home, slowly, one step, another step, and another.

That evening Papa and Mama drove to town, they had to send letters and telegrams, all kinds of things had to be arranged. Papa drove himself. And Urip slept with Rick in her room, on her mat; she hadn't done that in a long time.

In the middle of the night—the night light was burning —Rick awoke with a start and sat up straight in bed. What was it? What was it?

A sound, a voice, someone crying or singing aloud? Or an animal, a dog barking at the moon? No, no, it wasn't that.

Urip had got up; she listened with her neck stretched forward and her mouth open, then she leaned back against Rick's bed. "Buyung!" she said.

On the front veranda of the guest pavilion, Buyung was

sitting on his mat and singing the song of the dead. He sat with his knees drawn up and his arms around them, his head bent forward and sideways, his eyes closed, and while he sang he rocked back and forth. From deep down in his body a dull, dark sound arose, no melody, it went up and down on a few low notes, always the same.

It went up, and down again.

It swayed with his swaying body.

Loud, and then soft.

Rick was trembling in her bed; she was not afraid but she felt as if she had a pain somewhere which she couldn't bear. "Urip, Urip!"

Urip, leaning against her bed, held up her hand. "No," she said testily, "be still, listen, Buyung is talking with Mr. Fred."

Rick listened and after a while she thought that she understood what he said, that she could distinguish the words.

"Sir . . . sir," he said.

"Why did you go away—

"Sir—

"Why did you leave us—

"What have they done to you—?"

Always those same words.

But then the sound of the voice changed, became more emotional, faster, restless, Rick clasped her hands and whispered, "What is it, Urip?"

Urip shrugged. "Buyung must be looking for Mr. Fred."

"Uncle Fred, where are you?

"Buyung is looking for you, can't you hear?

"Uncle Fred, Uncle Fred, where are you?

"Are you still in the sea?" No, that couldn't be true.

"Near the sea? At sea perhaps, on a ship?

"Or are you still in Australia?

"Or are you here after all, here with us, with us?

"In the house or in the garden?

"In the guest pavilion? Buyung is waiting for you there. In your room?

"Or at the river with the boulders?

"Are you on the mountain, the Lawu? Near the crater? Near the lake? In the wood?

"Or at sea after all?"

It went so quickly, she didn't know anything could go so desperately fast as Buyung's voice, and she had to follow it.

"On the road to the town? At the river? On the big ferry? In the red ravine?

"At the Chinese tomb with the lions? In the little wood —the wood of that day, Uncle Fred?

"In the kanari driveway? Under the waringin tree, out in front?

"Or still in Australia? Australia?

"The sea? Which sea? One of the seven seas?

"Not with us after all?"

The voice echoed up and down, dull and desperate.

"Uncle Fred . . . Uncle Fred . . . where are you? Buyung is looking for you!"

And on and on went the voice, the whole night through.

Rick sat up in bed, trembling sometimes. Urip sat still on her mat.

It was warm that night, and dark outside. Nothing moved.

But finally, finally it seemed to cool off a little, the wind rose, there was the sound of water running in the ditches of the garden, and from somewhere came a bit of late moonlight.

Buyung still sat huddled, arms around his knees, but now he held his head up, farther back, and it was as if his voice didn't come from the depths of his body but from higher up, from his throat or his mouth.

He was still swaying, but not much, he sat almost still, his eyes wide open, staring into the moonlight—"Sir, sir, is that you, sir?"

The voice, soft, like a whisper, mounted, stopped, mounted, stopped.

Urip held up her hand. "Sshh."

The voice fell silent.

And it was still and cool in the early morning. Urip took her sirih box, folded the leaves, added some betel nut, and started to chew quietly. Rick lay down, her head on the pillow, she pulled the other pillow up against her face, it was over now, she could lie down and go to sleep.

FOR A SHORT WHILE IT SEEMED as if life would go on at the big house just as before, as if not so much had really changed. Only that the old gentleman was dead, and Uncle Fred, and Rose (but there was a new one in her place); that Aunt Nancy no longer came, and that Buyung would now remain their coachman.

Rick saw a lot of Buyung. She walked over to the carriage house when he was polishing the harnesses, or to the stables when he was grooming the horses. First he went on quietly with his work, then he might come over and talk to her about Uncle Fred. He would say, "Mr. Fred doesn't only like riding, he also likes the sea, sailing, or long marches through the jungle, his legs have to be bandaged tight against the leeches, they're wicked, very wicked!"

Or: "When Mr. Fred is hot and tired he loves to drink coconut milk."

Or: "Mr. Fred catches cold easily, and then I have to rub him with medicine." Simple daily things, as if Uncle Fred were still living. But after a while Buyung would get nervous and go away. In the afternoon at tea time, when the day's work was done, Buyung always sat with Mangun on the little bamboo bench in front of the lamp room. None of the others would dare go sit on that bench, just the two of them. Mangun was small and thin in his starched white trousers and jacket, his neatly folded kerchief; his skin wasn't very brown any more, dark ivory rather. He sat there still and lost in thought. And next to him Buyung, dark and untidy and heavy, hunched over with his legs up, the way Jimmy the ape sometimes sat. As a matter of fact, he looked a lot like Jimmy, with his protruding mouth, flat nose, and sad black eyes deep in their sockets. When he moved the whole bench creaked, and he shifted all the time because there was no peace in him.

They didn't talk much with each other, a few sentences about small things, about the tobacco being bad and much too expensive or something like that; and they always called each other "friend." That sounded nice and at the same time a bit solemn.

With the other servants Buyung spoke hardly at all. He and Urip never even looked in each other's direction, and he never gave a circus performance any more.

And life wouldn't go on as before. All the changes came

one after another. First, late one evening, Urip announced that she wanted to leave. Old Urip, where would she want to go? Papa had a talk with her, and Mama too, but she didn't listen, she didn't even say "perhaps" just to be polite; she just said point-blank, "no."

Was it because of Buyung?

"No."

Was she getting too old?

"No."

Did she no longer feel at home in the big house?

No, that wasn't it.

Didn't she like Rick any more?

"The miss has other people now," but that wasn't it, that didn't matter.

"Is there something else, then?"

"No, there's nothing else."

All with the same dark, inimical, closed face.

And when she came to say goodbye—after so many years—she still had that same fixed expression.

"Goodbye, sir, goodbye, madam, goodbye, miss," and in a formal, measured voice, "happiness to those who stay behind."

"Goodbye, Urip, happiness to those who go." Nothing else; only the nieces Assi and Nèng, whom she was taking with her, were standing there huddled together and crying hard.

And shortly after her departure the old coachman suddenly reappeared as if someone had sent for him. Buyung put on his ceremonial clothes once more and went to tell Papa that the old coachman was well again and that he assumed he could leave now. Papa flared up, Buyung was the best coachman they'd ever had, were they all going out of their minds? Buyung remained impassive under the torrent of words, he didn't say much. Only at the end, when Papa shouted at him, "But what do you want, then? You aren't from around here, you don't know a soul here, where do you want to go?" he said slowly, "Forgive me, sir, I did want to ask you for traveling money, I wanted to go back to . . . to . . . Mr. Fred."

This made Papa even angrier; he kept turning his head from side to side as if he wanted to shake off something. "But what kind of idiotic nonsense is that? Where do you think that . . ."

And the same hesitant voice: "I thought . . . perhaps, in my country . . . on Sumatra . . . perhaps . . ."

Then Papa shouted, and his voice trembled, "Look at me, Buyung. Mr. Fred is dead—dead—you know that!"

Buyung didn't look at him. "Certainly," he said quietly. "Buyung knows, of course Mr. Fred is dead." He didn't say more, there was nothing more to say, and Papa gave him his pay and the traveling money.

He didn't come to say goodbye, and they didn't see him leave—nobody did. One afternoon at tea time, Papa wasn't home, Mangun came to say that Buyung had already left, that he sent his respects and that he . . . and the usual good wishes followed. Then Mangun asked which horses should be harnessed for the afternoon drive.

"The dappled team," Mama said, as if everything were quite normal.

"You'll have to go alone, for I'm not coming," Rick said. When Mama answered, Rick became very impertinent and as a punishment had to go to bed an hour earlier than usual although she was a big girl. But she didn't care, and she didn't go on the drive with Mama.

While she was sitting alone at the big table eating her dinner, Mangun, who served her, said, "Why are you like that? It's good that Buyung returns to his own country, he is at home there, that's where he always was with Mr. Fred. You are being punished for nothing." He brought her some rice with dry-fried chicken from lunch, secretly, for he wasn't supposed to.

And when Rick was lying in bed behind the gauze curtains, an hour earlier than on other days—she was still very wide awake—staring at the room in the gleam of the night light, she folded her hands and without closing her eyes began to say her evening prayer, the Lord's Prayer. She said it almost mechanically, without being conscious of the meaning of the familiar words. And at the same time she saw—or was she dreaming, or just imagining it?—but she saw, like a painting on the wall, a wood.

A wood on Sumatra, jungle, nothing but trees, dark, tall, all growing together, with vines and lianas hanging down in loops and streamers. There was a trail and Buyung was walking along it. He was wearing his ceremonial dress, the stiff sarong in dark blue and gold pulled up over his waist with a big knot; underneath, the long black trousers; a black jacket with long sleeves; and the blue-and-gold kerchief with the two points behind one ear. He looked so dignified and even heavier and more solid than usual. A little behind him and to the side Uncle Fred was coming.

They walked quietly, not fast and not slow, for they were not going anywhere. They didn't speak. There was a cool green light around their heads.

In and around the trees, in the darkness of the wood, were beautiful gaudy birds, and also other animals, an elephant, a tiger, monkeys, a big spotted snake, perhaps a unicorn, and also a horse. The animals didn't move, they stood still under the trees, they did not want to do any harm, they were just looking. And nothing could happen, because Buyung was there. Buyung and Uncle Fred together.

"Forever and ever, amen," Rick said, and unfolded her hands.

The following day Papa came home early for afternoon tea. That was unusual. He stirred his cup two or three times and looked at Mama, but Mama shifted something on the tea tray and didn't look back at him. Then he said, and he seemed very friendly, "Rick, we have discussed this before, it's high time for you to go to Holland, have girl friends and go to a good school. I can't leave, but you could travel with a nice family. You'd like that, wouldn't you?"

Suddenly Mama pushed the tea tray aside and looked at him.

"I've told you, my only child isn't going to travel with strangers!" she said curtly. Rick had never seen her like that. Papa looked at Mama too; at first he was angry, but then he wasn't any more.

"All right," he said, "as you like. I can't leave. You'll have to take her, then—because this business of hanging around and doing nothing except chat with the servants has to stop, is that understood?"

"Fine," Mama said. "I'll take her. You can make our reservations for the boat."

"As you like," he said again.

"More tea?" Mama asked.

"No, thank you," Papa said, pushing his chair back and standing up. It was about time for their walk; out on the lawn one of the gardeners was standing, holding Jimmy. Papa waited a moment to see if Mama was coming too, but she pretended not to notice; she took the pot and poured herself another cup of tea. Then he walked down the marble staircase alone. He unhooked Jimmy's chain, took the ape by the hand and went into the garden with it. Mama drank her tea quietly and looked at the trees.

Rick looked too, and suddenly she saw how alone he was walking there. Papa alone with that horrible brown Jimmy in the big garden, so tall and thin in his white suit with his little beard. One of the water carriers had put down his cans and stood watching him from a distance. Perhaps he was even laughing at him—some master, without even a human being to keep him company, without a woman even, only an ape!

Rick had always been a little afraid of Papa, but less of late, and now she wasn't afraid of him at all.

"Please, go to Papa!" she said to her mother. "He can't walk there alone!"

Mama was already standing up—had she seen it too? While she hastily went down the stairs, Rick came after her.

"Why don't you let me go with those other people?" Rick said. "I don't mind so much—but can I have a velvet winter coat?"

Mama stopped, turned around and looked at her, and then she laughed. "All right, you'll have a velvet coat, and a velvet beret with a feather!" And suddenly they shook hands, just like that, right on the staircase. It seemed like a farewell, and it wasn't so terribly sad.

Mama walked on into the garden, toward Papa and Jimmy, and Rick turned and went through the house to the back veranda. At first she felt rather excited and pleased with herself, then that ebbed away.

Papa and Mama together, as always. She had given him Mama as a present—that wasn't wrong.

Now she was going away too. Like all the others—to die and to go away, it was the same.

Buyung yesterday.

And Uncle Fred; they were together now, they needed no one else with them.

Aunt Nancy of before—Riquette, Riquette: was that Rick after all?

And the old gentleman—she would never see the Dièng.

And Rose, poor Rose.

And Urip, who had always called her "heart of mine," but no more.

And Assi and Nèng.

And now she was going.

She was standing on the open veranda near the stairs. There was no one there. Twilight came, the sun was setting as always and its rays fell, not very warm, not very bright any more, into the green garden. The mountain stood beyond the wall, dark blue and broad, as always; the sky was so high and vast over the many rustling trees.

She stood there for some time, and she heard a rustling in a mangga tree on her left. It was Rose's white cockatoo which had perhaps plucked out her soul; it came down to the end of one branch with little lopsided jumps and eyed her curiously. Every now and again it made a sharp grating sound, raised its tuft of feathers, bent its head forward and asked impatiently to be scratched. Rick was glad with it there, she liked to feel its warm skin under the feathers.

A little later Mangun came through the garden looking for the cockatoo, which had to be put in its cage for the night. When he came closer and saw Rick, he turned toward her and asked, "What has happened?"

"I'm going away, Mangun," she said, "to Holland, on a ship."

"On a ship?" he asked. "On the sea?" There was great respect in his voice; he was from mid-Java, from the land between the mountains; he had probably never seen the sea. He stood still, thoughtfully; Rose's cockatoo had flown off the branch and lit on his shoulder.

"Just don't be afraid of the sea," he said after a while, "and you'll land safely. Don't be afraid!"

And it was as if the voyage were already over, as if her new friends were waiting on the quay, waving at her; as if she had to go ashore in Holland in a moment. But she couldn't do that, she wasn't there yet, she was still here. How could she look so far ahead? She had to stop and look back first.

There was so much: besides the people, the things she loved—her place on earth until then—the big house with the white marble floor and the black star, and the golden birds on the screens, the green walled garden, all the trees, all the flowers, the mountain—the Lawu beyond the garden wall. All the other mountains, the whole list, she had learned them all by heart.

Java and its blue mountains, and the blue sea around it. In the north the Java Sea, in the south the Pacific; to the left the Sunda Strait, to the right the Madura Strait, as they were on the map in the schoolroom.

She needed time to lose it all.

ABOUT THE AUTHOR

MARIA DERMOÛT, *who now lives in Holland, was born on a sugar plantation in central Java in 1888—the child of what was called in those days a colonial family. She was married at 18 and spent the next twenty-seven years on the islands of Java, Celebes, and the Moluccas, where her children and grandchildren were born. The Ten Thousand Things, Mme Dermoût's first full-length novel, written at 67, was a critical and popular success around the world. Yesterday, a fictional memoir of the author's girlhood in Java, appeared in Holland when Mme Dermoût was 63. It was her first published book.*

ABOUT THE TRANSLATOR

HANS KONINGSBERGER *has won high praise from the critics for his first novel,* The Affair, *and for his translation of Maria Dermoût's* The Ten Thousand Things, *both published in 1958. He was born in Amsterdam, has lived in New York since 1952, and is now at work on his second novel.*